The Country Singer

The Country Singer

ROBYN LEE BURROWS

Woman's Day Fiction

Copyright © 2005 Robyn Lee Burrows

First published in Australia in 2005 as a Woman's Day book by

ACP Publishing Pty Ltd

in association with Selwa Anthony and Mark Macleod

All rights reserved. No part of this publication may be reproduced, stored in a retrieval system, or transmitted in any form or by any means without the prior written permission of the publisher, nor be otherwise circulated in any form of binding or cover other than that in which it is published and without a similar condition being imposed on the subsequent purchaser.

All characters in this publication are fictitious and any resemblance to real persons, living or dead, is purely coincidental.

National Library of Australia
Cataloguing-in-Publication data

Burrows, Robyn, 1953-
  The country singer

  ISBN 1 86396 464 9

  I. Title. (Series : Woman's day (Sydney, N.S.W.))

A823.3

Cover photography: Getty Images
Cover design: David Kemp cthonic design

ACP Publishing Pty Ltd
54 Park St
Sydney NSW 2001
Phone: +612 9282 8618
fax: +612 9267 9438
www.womansday.ninemsn.com.au

For my special friend who believes life's a journey and not a destination, that there's magic in candles and that in every end there is a new beginning…

If you can dream –
and not make dreams your master

RB

CHAPTER 1

Coming home

2005
The wheat fields, Western Australia

I close the book with a snap and glance out the window. The mail plane is banking now, dropping lower, engine racing. Below, the landscape stretches away and the heat wavers upwards to the sun, pouring itself into the space between horizon and sky.

I can see the silver-beige wheat fields stretching as far as that same horizon and beyond, the road cutting a swathe through them. It is straight and narrow, the road, and flanked by a wobbly row of telegraph poles. Further back lie the railway line and a river that reflects the sky like a mirror. In contrast to the road, the river bends and twists itself across the flat landscape towards the sea. From this height it looks like a writhing snake.

The plane drops lower and I can feel the descent in the pit of my stomach. I've been sitting in this cramped seat for several hours now, watching the scenery speed by underneath, becoming drier and flatter, more remote. Now Jack the pilot reaches over, taps my arm and nods downwards. A cluster of trees and roofs swings into view. 'Almost there, Gemma,' he yells above the noise of the engine. I stretch my legs to prepare for our landing.

It's been years since I last visited. I close my eyes and mentally tally them. Six or seven, perhaps? Aunt Connie's sixtieth birthday. No, I think savagely, dismissing my calculation. How could I be so wrong? Connie turned seventy-two last spring. Twelve years! Where has the time gone?

I drove last time – a full day's journey from Perth that exhausted me. Since then, I've seen them – both Connie and my father – many times, but always in the city. Every summer I've sent them tickets and waited at the airport as they stumble off the plane, watching anxiously as they navigate the chaos that suburbia has become. They always look lost, and small, among the tall buildings and whizzing cars. Out-of-kilter. Dislocated. After a week or so, they always seem glad to be off.

I open my eyes. Wings dip, then straighten, sunlight glinting on the paintwork. As the mail plane drops lower I can see the township, briefly rumpling the flatness, grey and dusty in the heat, the school yard with children pointing upwards, hands shielding their small faces from the glare.

Silos – cylindrical concrete monoliths, black and shadowless – reach up above the trees, baking under the noon sun. General store and post office. Pub. Service station.

This is home.

A momentary sense of completeness – of familiarity with this place where I was born – overwhelms me. I blink and close my eyes again, letting the sensation take hold. Then, without warning, the reason for this unexpected visit slams back into my awareness.

Grady Halloran: my father.

Dead from a heart attack at seventy-five.

Old Horace from the general store is waiting by the long strip of tarmac as I tackle the mail plane's rickety steps. He's known me since I was a child.

'Hey, girlie, good to see you back again,' he says softly, awarding me an almost toothless grin as he holds out one gnarled hand and shakes mine. 'Connie sent me,' he adds simply, 'to bring you home.'

'Connie?' I ask, thinking of my lovable but cantankerous old aunt – Grady's sister. 'Where is she? I thought she'd be here to meet me.'

Horace frowns and glances away towards the long grass that borders the airstrip. A gust of hot wind has come up, bringing with it several round prickly bushes that bowl merrily along the nearby ridge of tar. 'Ah,' he says, spinning the word out in the slow way of country folk. 'There's been a slight hiccup where Connie's concerned.'

I fight a sudden lurch in my belly and I place my hand on his arm. 'What's wrong with my aunt?'

Horace looks down at my hand. 'The old biddy's too damn independent for her age, if you ask me. She had a bad fall yesterday and now she's in hospital with a broken leg. But she's sent firm instructions that you're not to worry. We can stop by there on the way, if you like.'

He lays my suitcase in the back of the ute and I climb into the cabin. It's a trusty workhorse with wheat heads scattered all over the floor and the lingering smell of pigs' food. The vinyl seat is torn and Horace grinds the gears as we go. *Clunk. Clunk.*

It labours noisily along the road, swaying from side to side as he steers around several large potholes. 'The old girl hates the heat,' he says and I nod, wondering vaguely if he's talking about Connie or the ute.

But I'm not bold enough to ask.

Past the few scattered buildings we go, towards the hospital on the outskirts of town. We pass the local service station with its doors and windows boarded up. The once-red petrol bowser is now a faded pink. Weeds sprout randomly along the edge of the concrete. The sight of the building, dismal and deserted in the glare, brings with it a fresh surge of grief. Grady's place.

I take a deep breath and close my eyes against the view, blocking the thought. I bring my fingertips to my temples and push back the pain that wells up inside me.

'You okay?' asks Horace and the car lumbers to a halt in front of the hospital.

I nod. If I speak, I know I'll cry.

Aunt Connie's lying in her hospital bed. There's some sort of cage under the bedclothes and the sheet humps up in a small mountain over the place where I imagine her leg is. She reaches out a hand and clasps mine.

'Gemma, dear,' she says and her voice sounds papery with disuse. 'I'm so glad you came.'

Three years younger than my father, Connie's seventy-two now. She looks frailer than when I saw her last, thin and old, reminding me again of the passing of the years and the way I've always thought the two of them will simply be there – my father and his sister. My only family.

'Of course I came.' I squeeze her hand lightly. Despite the heat of the day, her fingers feel cold and I bring them to my cheek, thinking to infuse some warmth into them.

'And look what I've done!' Her voice wavers as she points with her other hand towards the hump in the bed. 'So stupid, really. I was standing on a chair, trying to change a light bulb. Don't know what came over me. Dizzy, I suppose. Next thing I know – I've fallen. Three hours, it was, until someone came and found me.'

I picture her lying on the floor, unable to move without help. Accidents like this mean that old people should never live by themselves.

'Well, I'm sure they'll take good care of you here.' I pat the bed cover. 'You just relax and get better.'

But Connie's mind is already on other matters. 'You'll find Grady's house a mess, I'm afraid, dear. I was always asking him to clean it up a bit, or to let me do it. But he could never be bothered, especially after your mother died...'

Her voice breaks and she wipes a tear surreptitiously from the corner of her eye. 'Damn,' she mutters. 'I promised myself I wouldn't start crying in front of you.'

'Hey,' I try to jolly her out of her mood. 'It's all right, really.'

'Then when you went away to the city, Grady totally gave up, I guess,' she goes on, ignoring my reassurance. 'But you already know all that.'

I blink back sudden tears at her words. Is that how she saw my leaving this town: as a desertion?

But Connie can't see my wretchedness. She plucks distractedly at the edge of the sheet. 'The funeral,' she murmurs and I strain forward to hear her. 'It's not for a few days. I don't want to miss that.'

'Of course you won't. We'll borrow a wheelchair, or something. Don't worry.'

Appeased, she closes her eyes and I watch the rise and fall of her chest. Is she sleeping? I wonder. I wait a few minutes and then leave.

Horace is waiting for me outside, leaning against the side of the ute. 'How is the old girl?' he asks.

'Fair. She's fair.'

My gaze slides to my expensive suitcase in the back of the ute. Already it's covered in a fine layer of dust.

Horace takes me home. Back through the town we go, down long-familiar streets. From the front of Grady's house I stare across the paddock at the service station, seeing it differently for the second time that day. Faded sign – *Halloran's Service Centre. Est. 1955* – the words barely discernable. Paint-peeling bowser, sand piling up in drifts against the rusting metal sides. The bowser hasn't been used for years, not since the major oil company built the swanky new service station up at the crossroads, ten kilometres out of town, effectively putting Grady out of business. He only survived – or earned a bit of spending money – by doing minor mechanical repairs for a few faithful locals.

'Well, then,' Horace says, breaking my train of thought. 'Guess I'd better be going.'

He lifts my suitcase out and carries it into the house. The front door isn't locked, simply closed. It's a custom that jars with me, used as I am to city living, where everything is not merely locked, but dead-bolted and security screened as well.

He dumps the suitcase on the kitchen table with a grunt. 'Let me know if you need anything,' he offers with a tentative smile. 'And I wish it was better circumstances bringing you home, girlie.'

I nod. 'Thanks, Horace. Thanks for everything.'

The front screen door slams behind him and I hear his boots clunking the full length of the verandah, the sound becoming fainter with each step. Sunlight spears in an uncurtained window. From outside, I can hear the warble of a magpie.

Inside, nothing moves. It's as though time is standing still, suspended between past and present, reluctant to embrace the future. I hear the ute as it grinds its way back along the road, with the now-familiar *clunk-clunk* of the gears.

CHAPTER 2

A step out of rhyme

Nothing moves in the kitchen except for a handful of dust motes dancing in a stray beam of sunlight. The refrigerator hums. Grady's radio, strangely silent, sits on the bench. For an uncertain amount of time I stand there, not knowing what to do next. Minutes pass, each one blurring into the next, the time marked only by the slow methodical ticking of a clock. It chimes twice and I shake my head, thinking I should do something, anything, to take my mind from the hours and days ahead. The funeral; clearing Grady's effects from the house: these tasks I'm certainly not looking forward to.

I glance around the room. There are unwashed plates and coffee cups in the sink. I flick the knob on the radio, letting the room fill with the sudden static sound of the announcer's voice.

'In the west it'll be fine and dry, with the wind coming from the southeast…'

I fiddle with the knob, searching for music, and hit on a rap number spoken with a staccato beat, which sounds somewhat out of place here. Then I turn on the tap and squirt some dishwashing liquid under the gush of water. When the plates and cups are washed, I dry them and place them back in the cupboard.

I wipe my damp hands against the side of my jeans and stare at the floor. The lino – large yellow and black squares – was probably the height of fashion when it was laid some time before I was born. Now, near the back door, it's torn and lifting and I have the sudden sense of it peeling away like the layers of my heart. I stifle a wry smile, remembering Grady the last time I was home, standing in the kitchen with a bucket and a mop, taking ineffectual stabs at these same squares and cursing under his breath.

There's a small pile of unopened envelopes lying on the laminex-topped table, all addressed to him. I stare at his name for a moment. My father's gone yet these letters are still here, demanding attention and reminding me yet again of my loss.

I shuffle through them, as if they are a lousy hand of cards. On the front corner of one I can see the logo of the local electricity company, and there's a telephone account and a letter from Grady's bank. I prise them open with a sharp knife and lay the contents on the table. Paying bills for someone who is dead suddenly seems so pointless, and

I feel like tearing them up. But I know I won't. Instead I'll pay them, like a dutiful daughter, before I go back home.

My thoughts slide sideways to my own home. The one I live in, in my adult life, is a hip inner-city townhouse I share with Greg, my lover of five years. He's a wonderful guy, Greg. Outgoing and personable. Hard-working. Cute, too, in a rugged suntanned kind of way. He's in the music industry and runs a small recording studio, employing half a dozen staff. That's how we met. I'd been cutting a demo CD, hopeful of a break with my singing career. He asked me out to dinner and we went on from there.

I'm thirty-five. Greg's three years older. My music career's never really taken off, though I'm still optimistic. Greg says I just need the right song, something special. There's too much of the same style out there and I need a different sound, he says, something to make people sit up and take notice. So I'm still looking, and trying to pen a few tunes myself.

Greg wants to make our relationship permanent and he's ready to commit. Only last week he took me to a lovely restaurant overlooking the beach. The meal was superb, the service great. Then, a few minutes before we were due to leave, he took a small box from his pocket and I knew instantly what was about to happen.

'Marry me, Gem,' he said, offering it to me.

And all I could do was shake my head and whisper, 'I can't do this. I'm not ready.'

'When will you be?' he said quietly, placing the box back in his pocket. I saw immediately that I'd wounded him.

It's not that I don't love him: I do. We fit together like ying and yang, but the whole marriage and commitment thing scares me witless. Till death do us part. Promising undying love. Making vows that I can't guarantee to keep. You've only got to read the glossy women's magazines to see the flaws in that way of thinking. There's always some celebrity saying publicly that they've found the love of their life, only to separate or divorce three issues later.

Greg would probably say I'm just being flip, but over the years I've seen lots of my friends suffer through divorce. So I've come to the conclusion that emotions are only ever for the moment. The person you love today might not always be the one you love tomorrow. People change. Our expectations alter as we get older. So for now I'd rather keep my relationship with Greg as it is, and not complicate matters with marriage.

My mother, Meg, died when I was quite young, but I don't have childhood recollections of happiness in this house. I remember strained silences and reproving looks. There are a few smudged memories of her crying and Grady storming from the room. 'Why didn't you let me go?' she yells the words after my father as he slams the screen door behind him and walks away from her – and me – across the paddock.

The memory hurtles back, whether I want it or not. I see Grady as he was then, hunch-shouldered, a man seemingly bowed by pain. I take a deep breath. What place other than here would Meg Halloran rather have been? And if she had gone, would I, as her only child, have gone too?

I am the age my mother was when she had me, many years after her marriage. Grady told me once about all the babies she'd lost before me, and how each time he'd cried and held her and told her it didn't matter, that there'd be another time, the proper time, because for some unfathomable reason it wasn't meant to be, just yet. But inside it was eating him up too.

'It hurt, Gem,' he said, looking sad, dragging back the memories. 'To think of all those little wasted lives. Of the people they might have become, your brothers and sisters.'

Greg's ready to start a family and become a father. He comes from a large clan and loves kids. All his nieces and nephews think he's really neat and they enjoy spending time at our house. But for some reason I feel awkward around children. There's some sense that I don't quite fit in or relate; that I'm more a spectator than a player.

My mind slides back to last night and the minutes just before the phone call telling me about my father…

Greg's standing by the doorway to my study, saying, 'It'd be different with our own child. You'd make a great mother. Trust me.'

'Greg, please.'

I'm trying to finish a proposal in time for a staff meeting in the morning. I flash him a look of irritation.

'Just think about it. That's all I'm asking.'

I lay down my pen, lock my fingers into a steeple and rest my chin on them. 'Look, I don't really feel any urgency to be a mother and I wouldn't know where to begin being one. How are mothers supposed to act? How should they *be*? Tell me. My own childhood didn't exactly come with much instruction.'

'Gem, if we had a baby you'd be fine. A lot of women feel like you do.'

'Since when are you an expert on how women feel?'

He stares at me, unblinking, for one long moment. 'That's not fair,' he says.

'I'm just not ready for the motherhood thing, okay? And, what's more, I'm not certain if I ever will be. Can we just leave it at that?'

He raises both his hands, palms facing me in a gesture of defeat and surrender. Then he backs out of the room and closes the door firmly behind him.

He's right. The question isn't fair and I shake my head, feeling guilty and patronising and bitchy. My words were meant to wound and obviously they did.

I read once that what men want is to be adored and what women want is to be understood. And of all the people in the world, it's Greg who knows me best, who understands the real Gemma. He knows how scared I am, how terrified of trying and failing and of simply not knowing how to handle those things that seem to come naturally to most women. Marriage. Motherhood. That instinctiveness.

The telephone interrupts my thoughts and I pick it up. 'Gemma speaking,' I say, a little more brusquely than I'd intended.

'It's Aunt Connie here, love. I'm afraid there's some bad news.'

There's a tremor in her voice, a distinct wobble. My heart flip-flops. *Grady*, I know instantly. *It's Grady*. For a moment I can't speak, can't form logical thoughts. *Please, no.*

'Gemma? Are you there, dear?'

A long sigh escapes from my mouth. 'Yes, I'm here.' *Get it over with. Say the words quickly and perhaps they'll be less painful.*

'I'm sorry, Gemma. Grady's dead.'

I knew it. 'How? When?' I ask automatically, my mouth forming the words. They spin away from me uselessly, dissolve into air and silence, then into the sound of Aunt Connie crying miles away, already missing the brother with whom her life has been so intertwined...

I shake my head, bringing myself back to this house in the middle of the wheat fields and Grady's mail; to that yellow and black checked lino. Back to awful reality.

The door to Grady's bedroom is closed. I pause outside in the hallway and lay my forehead against the wall, fighting back tears for the umpteenth time today. Why do I keep pushing my grief to some place deep inside? What part of me won't let my emotions succumb to the pain? Maybe it's because I know that if I let myself, the tears may never stop until the core of me is hard and dry.

I go instead to the spare bedroom, which is musty with the odour of disuse. I throw open the window and lean out, taking in great lungfuls of air. Then I turn and look around me.

This room was mine in another lifetime, during my lost childhood. Now it looks smaller than I remember, the walls closer together. They are still bright pink. (How could I ever have thought the colour attractive?) I bend down and peer under the bed where dust balls scatter on the floorboards. Then I fall on the blue-and-white ticking of the mattress and stare morosely up at the ceiling.

A small patch of mould flowers in the corner, its tendrils spreading out insidiously and snaking across the plaster. I think about Grady and my mother, about the too short life they shared. I think about the way Aunt Connie took over after my mother's death.

'Good old Connie,' Grady used to say. 'She's a good old stick, looking after us like this. What'd we do without her?'

What indeed? But, I suppose now, we would have muddled on; got by somehow.

I think about Connie lying in her hospital bed, looking feeble and suddenly old. Why has she never married? What sense of duty made her devote her life to the raising of her niece and the care of her brother? Her mortality suddenly stares me boldly in the face. Will she be the next to go?

At dinnertime I sort through the contents of the pantry. There's not much to choose from: baked beans, tuna, creamed corn and condensed milk. Obviously Grady's been existing from one day to the next. I find some bread, rather stale, in the fridge and a chunk of cheddar. Then I prepare myself grilled cheese on toast and make a mental note to go down to the store in the morning and buy a few supplies.

The telephone jangles in the stillness of the house. It's Greg. 'Hi,' he says and his voice sounds distant.

'Hi, yourself.' There's a long pause. 'So, what's happening?' I ask at last, unable to bear the silence.

'Nothing much.'

He goes on to tell me a few things about the people at the office and a couple of messages of condolence left on my answering machine. I let the words wash around me, conscious again of the last few hours we spent together, the night of the phone call to tell me Grady had died, and the argument we had before it.

'When's the funeral?'

I shake my head, dragging myself back to the present. 'Friday.'

'I should come – be with you.'

'No!' I answer quickly. 'I can handle this by myself.'

Why don't I want him here? Greg scarcely knows – *knew* – Grady. They'd only met a few times in the city; two men about as different as you could get. One, a country bloke, rough around the edges with a heart as big as the moon. The other –

I close my eyes, trying to even out my breathing.

'Goodbye, then,' says Greg. 'I love you, Gem,' he adds, but he sounds hesitant, as though unsure of the words, or what I might say in reply.

'Bye,' I answer mechanically and hang up.

Afterwards, I sit out on the front step, the memory of the phone call fresh in my mind. There's a chirp of night crickets, the distant barking of a dog. Away to my left, the lights from nearby houses wink back at me. Other people's lives are going on while mine seems at a standstill.

I remember Greg's parting remark as I boarded the mail plane earlier in the day. 'I love you, Gem,' he said, but the words now feel like dead wood washing up on a distant shore.

I lose track of how long I sit there in the dark, rehashing my thoughts. Random memories of growing up here as a child appear without warning. Long hot summer days. The whirr and hum of harvesters churning through the wheat and the sweet smell of rain falling on dust. My first day at school. The local pool on endless tiring days. Baubles on the Christmas tree.

The sound of a car comes and goes. I shiver and wrap my arms around myself, feeling suddenly alone. This is Grady's place – no longer mine. I'm not the same person I was when I lived here, and the memories belong to another time.

'Stop it!' I mutter, noting that most of the lights in the street have gone out. This town, I'd forgotten, is one of early risers. I go inside and lock the door behind me, although there's no reason to. What could happen out here? It's a city instinct, locking doors and windows, shutting other people out of our lives. Like what I'm doing to Greg.

Inside the house I flick on the switches and flood the old rooms with light.

'I want marriage, a family,' he'd said to me last night.

'All the traditional trimmings,' I'd bantered back. 'A mortgage. Two-and-a-half kids.'

'We've already got the mortgage,' he'd reminded me quietly. 'And what's so wrong with tradition?'

'Nothing,' I'd said, suddenly quiet, as a childhood image of my mother hit me. Meg, my mother, standing in the doorway of the service station, hands on hips, yelling at Grady. I see the way her mouth twists, see the pain in her face and hear the resentment in her voice.

'Connie should have left me there!' she yells, the words rushing at me out of the past, raw and shocking. 'She should have let me go.'

Next morning, I go into Grady's room. I can no longer put the moment off and I don't want to. I stand, looking at the bed. The blanket is thrown back, the sheets a horrible grey colour. The shape of his head still marks the pillow. I fight back the knowledge that this is the room where my father died; that between those sheets he took his last breath.

Tears well up in my eyes. He will never again sleep in this bed, will never know the feel of cotton beneath his skin. A pain stabs me in the chest, so acute that, for a moment I think I might cry out with the intensity of it.

I rip the sheets from the mattress, bolt from the room and throw them by the back door. Later I'll light the incinerator and burn them until they are reduced to ash.

Back in the bedroom, a framed photograph on the dressing table catches my eye. I pick it up and stare at the scant remembered features. Dark hair framing her oval face. Slightly upturned nose. She's standing with her hands on her hips, smiling boldly at the camera. The pose is both seductive and challenging. *Catch me if you can.*

My mother: Meg Halloran.

She died when I was eight and sometimes I wonder if the few memories I have are real at all, or simply images of the way I *want* to remember her. Feeling the steady *thump-thump* of her heart as she rocks me to and fro, holding me against her breast. Running through the wheat as she places one hand across her eyes, shielding them from the sun and calling, 'Gemma, where are you? I can't see you.' And me trying not to laugh in case I give away my hiding spot.

My parents sitting in the living room after dinner, my mother knitting and Grady reading the newspaper. The silences between them.

Why do I always remember the silences?

I place the frame back on the dresser and open the nearby cupboard. I find old shoes, most carrying a layer of dust, and a suit frayed around the cuffs that I've never seen Grady wear. How old is this stuff? Probably older than I am.

After lunch, I go through the dresser, discarding ruthlessly. Holey socks and undies all end up in a large green plastic bag. They're not even fit for the charity bin outside the general store. Then in the bottom drawer there's a pile of paperwork: old electricity bills and cheque stubs. Several pens that no longer work. Paper clips. A pencil sharpener. The remains of two stubby candles and a small piece of agate.

At the bottom there's a sheet of paper. It's worn around the edges, as though it's been opened and refolded many times. I lay it on the top of the dresser and smooth the creases flat with the palm of my hand.

It's a music score, with words written underneath, but the words don't make sense. I read and re-read them, frowning as I try to work out what they mean.

Meg's Song
A moment, a fragment,
split second of time.
A dead love, a lost love,
a step out of rhyme.
We woke to the birdsong
a bright yellow dawn
that shone through our lives
when the dark night had gone

Puzzled, my mind skims the rest of the words. Then, right at the bottom, I read, 'The poetry is yours. The tune is mine. I've blended them with love. Declan.'

I fold the paper back up and put it in my pocket, aware that I've been holding my breath. I breathe out slowly and bring my hands up against my cheeks. What is the meaning of this? And why has Grady kept it in his bottom drawer?

I close the front door behind me and walk along the street in the direction of the hospital, holding back the impulse to run. The journey seems to last forever.

Aunt Connie is lying in her bed, in much the same position as yesterday. 'Gemma,' she says, a smile creasing her face as I walk into the room.

I take the paper from my pocket and hand it to her. She adjusts her spectacles and peers at the words, a frown of concentration on her face. When she finishes, she hands it back. Then she closes her eyes.

'Don't go to sleep on me, Aunt Connie,' I beg her.

'No, dear. I'm just thinking,' she says.

'I need to know.' I can hear the hard edge in my voice. 'Who's Declan?'

She opens her eyes and I see they are bright with tears. The wetness spills over her lids and rolls down her face. She blinks, closes her eyes again. 'Gemma,' she says, 'there's something you should know.'

I lean forward, waiting. 'Yes?' I say breathlessly.

Her words are a long time coming. She seems to be summoning them from somewhere deep inside her head. Then, at last, she stares at me.

'There are certain things about your mother I've always thought you should have been told,' she whispers, her mouth twisting.

Something inside me lurches, then rights itself.

'The truth, Aunt Connie,' I say. 'Just tell me the truth.'

CHAPTER 3

Long, lonely miles

1969
The wheat fields, Western Australia

Beyond the silos and trucking yards, the land stretches flatly away, the horizon quivering like jelly in the heat. The pub and post office and general store stand baking in the sun. Out the front of the service station, the petrol pump is fading, the paint starting to peel away in long flaky shards. A dog lies in the shade of a nearby tree, panting and swishing at flies with its tail. At one end of the small railway siding, washing flaps from a makeshift line strung from one of the disused railway carriages where the fettlers camp.

It is September in the Western Australian wheat fields. From outside the small cottage, across the paddock from the local service station, Meg Halloran imagines she can hear the wind coming from long, lonely miles away, can hear the moan of it past the scrubby stand of bonewood as she hangs the washing on the line – two of Grady's shirts, a pair of trousers and her knickers – and turns her head to the trucking yards and the direction of the imaginary sound. A dog barks and the hot breeze gusts towards her.

Only Spring, she thinks, running the back of her hand across her brow and finding it damp, *and so hot*.

Already she's dreading summer.

'Meg!'

Grady's insistent voice rattles towards her from inside the house. She should be in there, she knows, packing the clothes for her husband's trip. The truck, a World War 2 vintage Chevrolet, will be here soon to collect him.

Grady is the local mechanic. He's owned the only service station in town for fourteen years. *"Halloran's Service Centre. Est 1955"* says the sign that hangs above the bowser.

Today he's going further west, to one of the big properties. There's machinery to be repaired and maintenance to be done on the farm vehicles. It's an annual trip and he'll be gone for at least a week. Meg has been looking forward to his absence with guilty pleasure.

She'll have seven days of being by herself, of not having to fuss or worry. Seven days of preparing meals for one. A week of lazing in bed in the mornings with the stack of new books from the lending library in the next large town, delivered a week earlier by the mail plane. They have been in her cupboard since then, brought out only last night and placed beside her bed where Grady eyed them with mistrust.

'Don't know why you'd be wanting to fill your head with all that fah-de-dah,' he said, snatching back the bed covers with a savage pull. 'You'd be better off doing something sensible with your time.'

'Such as?'

She couldn't resist the question, which was rhetorical anyway. She already knew her husband's answer. So she turned her back on him and slid the night gown over her shoulders, hiding her nakedness and giving him the subtle message. Not tonight.

They've been married for fifteen years, she and Grady; got married a year before he bought the service station. He had high hopes for the place. *Halloran and Sons*, he's always planned to write on the sign. But that has never eventuated.

Meg has lived in this town since fifth grade, having arrived with her father from a big property further out, and this is about as close to civilisation as she's ever been. The drought wiped her father out and he died a broken and bitter man in a haze of alcohol. Her mother had disappeared years earlier.

Meg and Grady: childhood sweethearts. He's forty now, five years older than her, and they've been together since she was in high school. There was never going to be anyone else – at least that's what he has always told her. And when she turned eighteen he got down clumsily on one knee and asked her to marry him. No great flowery speech or declaration of love, though. Just a simple 'Marry me, Meg.'

He would take her from the misery of her life – at least that's what he promised. Two years later they wed in the little church and all the townsfolk turned out to wish them well.

Fifteen years! She lets her mind slide back through the memories, sorting images, filing them in their proper order. Grady in his suit on their wedding day. The week-long honeymoon at the next large town along the railway line. Making love with him that first time, all awkwardness and arms and legs and embarrassed silences, touching, exploring in the dark. Grady holding his hand over her mouth saying, 'Sshh, sshh,' though she wasn't certain who he thought might hear as she cried into the night. Learning to cook on the cantankerous stove in the cottage that had belonged to his parents before them. The babies she's lost.

Those fifteen years have not lived up to Meg's expectations. She thought then, naively, that marriage meant intimacy, and those precious tender shared moments she's read about in books, when a man holds a woman and tells her how much he loves her and says he would lay down his very life for her.

But Grady, she has discovered with the passage of time, is a man of few words or emotional demonstrations. His days are spent tinkering with the cars in the service station workshop. Most of his nights are spent propping up the bar at the little hotel next to the railway siding. And their lovemaking, the only space where their lives have ever touched, now leaves her breathless for other reasons.

Apart from Connie, Grady's sister, there's no other woman she feels comfortable talking to. Her own mother has long since gone and her childhood school friends now live in the city. Sometimes this town seems filled with old people.

She longs to have a conversation with her husband that isn't about the price of wheat or the lack of rain. She wants to discuss the things she reads about in the books, to ask him if he sometimes looks at the moon and wonders why it doesn't fall from the sky, or if he ever smells the wind as it blows in from the river, sweet and dry. She's vaguely aware that some vital part's missing in her life, or in both their lives, and it reminds her of something lost or forgotten – or perhaps some vague emotion she's never experienced in the first place, although she longs to.

She hears the sound of the wind again, or thinks she does, and, holding one hand across her eyes to shield them from the sun, scans the paddocks that stretch away flatly before her.

The wheat is almost ripe. It's Durum mostly, sown in autumn and harvested in spring. In a few weeks time the teams of combine harvesters will arrive and they'll thresh through those same fields, day and night.

She likes night-time harvesting the best. Grady's usually at the pub or hunched over his bookwork, so she sits on the back step and listens to the drone of the huge machines, their lights cutting a dazzling swathe through the darkness, skimming the top of the wheat which looks like a bright moving sea.

'*Meg!*'

Grady's voice, more insistent now. She glances up and sees the old Chevvy heading towards her down the dirt road and kicking up a cloud of dust.

'Coming,' she calls as she sprints to the house and the room where she shares those long nights with him.

CHAPTER 4

Shameful little secret

After Grady leaves, Meg takes a slim volume of poetry from her collection of books and settles in her favourite position on the steps at the front of the cottage. Until the night before, when she let him see them, the books have been stowed away in her side of the bedroom cupboard for a week, hidden from him like some shameful little secret that has to stay that way until he goes.

From time to time she's slid open the cupboard door and eyed them eagerly. Grady didn't get past fourth grade at school and can't understand her preoccupation with the written word. He hates it when she 'has her nose stuck in a book', and he often tells her so.

Now that he's gone, Meg can indulge herself and not have to bear his taunts and complaints.

She holds the book of poems, pressing the spine against her cheek, delaying the moment when she turns the pages and begins to read. The book feels warm and somehow alive. The anticipation has been building up for days and it will waken within her new words and images. Sitting on the step in the shade and watching the road that unravels its way past the cottage, she savours the feeling.

The road is white gravel and the sunlight glares off it. A gust of wind barrels along the fence line, pulling several small burry bushes in its wake. The cottage is a mile down the railway line from the siding, and over the top of the wheat field she can see the shape of the three silos against the sky, the outlines dark and quivering in the heat. She blinks and closes her eyes for a moment against the sight, emptying her head of thought. Then she opens the book to the first page and lets the rhyme and rhythm of the words wash over her.

Declan O'Brien pulls the truck to a shuddering stop in front of the petrol bowser. He calls it a truck – it's big and bulky and has carried him over many a country road – though some might say it's more like an overgrown ute: a Ford F100.

Anyway, for the past few hours he's been carefully nursing it over rough and bumpy roads, ears tuned for the noise. Perhaps it's the motor, or the gearbox: he's not certain. Mechanics has never been his strong point.

The noise started as intermittent rattle and progressed to a steady *kerthunk*. As the miles have gone by he's become increasingly concerned, wondering if the thing will even make it to the next town.

He's found this place by getting off the main highway up at the big T-intersection, taking the back roads and following the signs. Purposefully he's slowed, changing back a gear, and the dirt track has crawled interminably under him. At last, when he saw the silos – three, he counted – and the grain elevator materialise out of the bush, he knew that help was close.

Now, relieved, he clicks open the truck door and steps out into the midday heat. It comes at him in waves, the heat, roiling upwards from the red-baked earth. He feels it burning at his face then he senses a trickle of perspiration down his neck. The back of his shirt is already damp.

Nothing moves. There's no breeze; not even a hint of one. Even the leaves on the trees are still. He glances about, somewhat disappointed but taking in the scene. The petrol bowser, probably once bright red, has faded, as though the heat has leached the colour from the paint. Weeds sprout randomly along the edge of the concrete driveway. The sign above the front door reads *"Halloran's Service Centre. Est. 1955"*.

There's no one about. The door under that same sign is shut and Declan senses it is locked as well. The building has a general air of abandonment, indicating that the owner is not merely at lunch or under the bonnet of a nearby car, but is not close by at all.

Damn! He's been relying on the repairs here to get him going again, but it doesn't look promising.

He thinks for a moment, then leans into the cabin of the truck and presses his hand on the horn, twice. Perhaps the sound will summon help. He paces the length of the vehicle, scanning the landscape for some movement – anything – a sign that someone has heard. A shout perhaps, a muttered curse. A hang-on-a-moment-will-you-mate-I'm-coming.

But nothing moves. There's no sound to break the silence except for the *tick-tick* of the truck engine as it cools, so he strides back to the open door and leans on the horn again.

Meg hears the sound of a car horn coming from the direction of the service station: two short bursts, a silence, then one more. It seems like a summons, the horn, and an intrusion. Before her, the words fly off the page, taking themselves out of her mind and her memory. She cannot remember a single one of them.

'Okay! Okay!' she mutters to herself.

With a sigh, she closes the book, gets up and leans against the verandah post as she scans the landscape stretching away before her.

Her attention is drawn to the service station. She can see a small truck – one she's never noticed before – parked next to the petrol bowser. A man paces up and down beside it. He's wearing jeans, she can see from this distance, and a checked shirt: green and white. From the way he's walking she senses his irritation. Frowning, she walks into the midday sun and makes her way towards him.

As she approaches, the man leans over the bonnet. He has a map spread across its surface and he's studying it, for a moment unaware of her presence. She is looking into the sun, so she raises one hand to shield her eyes.

'Are you after someone?' she calls.

He swings round and his body is framed by the open truck door, the outline a dark smudge in the glare. Meg cannot make out his expression, but is simply aware of his height and the width of his shoulders, the long tapering shape of him and the impression of a hat.

'Grady,' he says. 'I'm looking for Grady Halloran.'

She's walking as he speaks, coming closer. Now, mere feet away, she can see him clearly for the first time. He's tall, even taller than her first impression, and instantly she's aware of his eyes as they focus on her. Blue eyes, she thinks, the colour reminding her of the sky just before a storm. Dark blue. Almost indigo. Brooding. He nods in the direction of the sign above the service station door. 'Obviously I've come to the right place.'

Something about him takes the breath from her lungs. 'Yes,' she says, drawing air in through her mouth, the word coming out more brusquely than she's intended.

'I was sent here from the general store. The man there said to ask for Grady.'

There is a cadence to his words, a rhythm that sends them spinning past her into the air. For a moment, Meg can't speak. Then she searches for her voice and finds it. 'Grady's away.'

He stands there, saying nothing, though he is processing her statement. Then he wipes his forearm across his brow.

'Gosh, it's hot,' he says.

'You could say that.'

His eyes crinkle into life and suddenly the corners of his mouth curve upwards, creasing to match his eyes. 'Looks like its gearing up for a scorcher of a summer.'

The heat is a constant part of Meg's life, something she's not given much thought to lately and the locals have long-since stopped commenting on the weather. Hoping it was cooler is just like wishing for the moon, she thinks, then nods, unable to think of a single thing to say.

The man introduces himself. 'Declan O'Brien,' he says, offering her his hand. Tentatively she shakes it and his grip is firm, his fingers warm. 'My truck's playing up, has been for a few miles now. I need to get further down the line.'

'Where are you headed?'

He names the nearest town, several hours drive away.

'When do you need to be there by?'

'Oh, I reckon I've got a few days spare.' Declan O'Brien nominates a date almost a week away.

'You could probably walk it by then,' Meg says dryly, 'if you were that way inclined.'

'It'd be a thirsty trip.'

She's been studying him as he speaks. He's hard and lean, with a wide full mouth and dark hair that flops across his forehead. Beads of perspiration line his upper lip. There's a damp stain around his collar, the fabric of the shirt there darker than the rest. His skin is tanned and his eyes – smiling eyes, she thinks – squint against the glare. Tiny crease lines fan out from the corners, as though he's spent too many hours in the sun. Handsome, she supposes, in a rumpled, careless kind of way.

She's aware again of his hair and fights back a sudden impulse to brush it from his forehead and rearrange it more tidily. *Goodness*, she thinks, blocking the thought from her mind. She has never had thoughts like this before. Not about her husband Grady, anyway, and certainly never about a stranger.

A slow embarrassed flush creeps up her cheeks. In her moment of confusion, she hopes this man named Declan O'Brien hasn't noticed.

Haltingly she explains Grady's absence and says he won't be back for several days, maybe even a week.

'A week?'

'Well, that's only till he gets back. Then he might have to order parts for your truck, depending on what's wrong. That could take longer. The mail plane only comes twice a week with spare parts.'

He rubs his hand across his chin. 'Guess I'll have to look for somewhere to stay.'

'You could try the pub,' she offers. 'But I don't like your chances. Tomorrow's the annual local race day and the place is likely to be full.'

'So my luck's really run out.' He grins, patting the bonnet of the truck. 'Never mind. I've slept in this old girl before. It's a bit cramped, but at least it's free.'

Meg thinks of the distance this man has come and the miles he has yet to travel, and feels a sense of responsibility for his care and wellbeing. It's not his fault that his truck's broken down, or that there's no accommodation left in town. Just a rotten run of bad luck.

'Look, it's not much, but it's functional,' she says, hoping she won't regret the offer even as she says the words. 'There's a room at the back of the service station. You're welcome to stay. There aren't any cooking facilities, but the pub puts on a decent feed.'

Grady sometimes sleeps in the back room when he works late so he won't wake her by coming home. And although the bathroom is small it has a shower and toilet. It's nothing flash, but it's comfortable enough.

Declan O'Brien glances back at his truck. 'Seems I don't have a lot of choices.' He smiles ruefully. 'Thanks for the offer. I really appreciate it.'

There is a sincerity in his tone of voice that makes her feel easy inside and glad that she's made the suggestion. It's the least she can do, she supposes, since Grady isn't here to help the man. Declan O'Brien's use of the room will cost her nothing, and in a few days Grady will return and fix the truck and this stranger will be on his way, never to be seen again.

Declan moves the truck to a shady spot at the rear of Grady's service station. Then he reaches into the back of the cabin and hoists out a suitcase and a guitar. Meg raises her eyebrows at the sight of the guitar, but says nothing. It's none of her business, after all. Silently she leads him to the spare room and throws open the door.

'Okay, then,' she says, staring directly into his eyes and mentally daring him to look away. There's a sudden uncharacteristic boldness inside her, a sense of daring. 'I'll show you where the bed linen's kept.'

She steps into the room, goes across to the tall cupboard next to the window and takes out a pair of sheets and a pillowcase. Then she stands in front of the bed, and this time avoids his eyes. 'I can make it for you, if you like,' she offers.

'Thanks, but I'll be fine.'

'I don't mind, really.'

'This isn't a hotel. You don't have to wait on me.' He softens his words with a smile.

She waits, biting her lip again, unsure of his reply. 'Well, then,' she says. 'Lunch at the pub is from midday until two.' She points across the paddock to her own cottage, past the stand of bonewood. 'If you need anything, I'll be over there.'

'Thanks.'

She half expects him to turn away from her then, dismissing her, to attend to something – unpacking the contents of his suitcase perhaps. But he doesn't look away, at least not at first. He holds her gaze instead and it is she who blinks and averts her eyes, letting them slide downwards until they take in the threadbare patches in the carpet.

Suddenly she feels ashamed of this place, embarrassed that the floor covering should be so old and shabby, the furniture so worn. Perhaps he is used to finer things? Maybe he comes from a background of wealth and privilege? But then, what is he doing out here, miles from anywhere, driving this old truck?

Let it go! What is she thinking? And why does she suddenly feel so involved with a man she has only just met?

The question gnaws, then is gone. Not knowing, she turns and walks away, back to the shady step and the book of poems.

CHAPTER 5

Other Septembers

Declan stands in the doorway of the room behind the service station and surveys the tatty floor covering and unmade bed. He sees worn patches in the carpet and a large oil stain near his feet.

Sadly the furniture looks as though it's seen better days. The frayed blue-and-white ticking on the mattress stares back at him accusingly and he realises that the room is not so different from the one he's stayed in the night before, and the night before that. Closing the screen door behind Meg Halloran, he walks across the room and dumps his suitcase and guitar on the table.

What's he going to do in this place for a week? How will he fill time? He already knows what kind of town this is, without asking. Obviously there's no television this far out, and no picture theatre. He hasn't even brought a book to read.

'Damn!' he mutters softly to himself.

He's not a man of explosive temper; rather, there's a quiet building-up of frustration inside him, an air of unease. He'd rather be travelling than standing in this rarely used room with the worn and stained reminders of other people's lives. Too long he's been living like this, he acknowledges. Perhaps it's time he settled down again, found a place of his own. Maybe he's been too long on the road.

There's a stale smell to the room and he throws open the window, letting the grubby curtain billow inwards on the breeze. Then he lies on the bed with his hands under his head as he stares up at the ceiling.

The paint is peeling there, flakes hanging above him. He imagines them falling on him as he sleeps, layering across his eyes and nose until his face is covered and he is no longer visible. He could suffocate, he thinks, and then he checks himself. He's been living this solitary life too long, immersed in his own weird imaginings. Paint flakes? Come on! He needs to get out more, spend less time in lonely rooms like this one.

To the right, a spider's web loops its way across one corner of the room, linking the two walls, the carcasses of several flies caught in it. But there's no sign of the spider. In the distance, Declan hears a car stutter into life and in the trees outside a cicada begins its shrill call. A desultory breeze blows in through the open window. He closes his eyes, thinking of other rooms, other towns and other Septembers.

It was September when he first met Susan, on a day

not so unlike this one. Her father owned the local pub and he arrived in town, dusty from several hours travel. She showed him to his room. Up the stairs she went, in front of him, and as he walked behind her he noticed the swing of her hips and the way her dark auburn hair fell down past her shoulders, draping across them like a cape. Then, at the doorway, she turned and smiled, and he knew with sudden clarity that all his life he'd been searching for her and that somehow their futures would be entwined as surely as the links on the gold chain around her neck.

It was Susan who nicknamed him 'the country singer'. She said it first in a lilting, teasing voice, dusky with desire the first night he took her to his bed.

'All my life I've been waiting for you,' she added, kissing him hard until he thought his body might melt and dissolve into hers, so fully had she encompassed him, both physically and spiritually. 'Why did you take so long to find me?'

He didn't know how to reply.

Why indeed?

Surely there should have been a path, distinct and clear, leading him to her, but it seemed he had stumbled upon her accidentally and love had come suddenly and swiftly, without warning, catching him up in its force and carrying him along, a not-unwilling participant.

'I have nothing to give you,' he said, pressing her hand against his mouth. 'I've got no home, no regular job. Being on the road is a nomadic life.'

'Just give me yourself,' she said. 'That's all I need.'

'I love you,' he whispered later, after their passion had been spent and they lay on the rumpled sheets, arms and legs and hearts entwined. He ran his lips the length of her neck, taking in the sweet smell of her. Even now, years later, he still imagines he can taste her skin. 'With all my heart, I love you.'

And he meant it.

It was the following spring before they married. By that time she'd accompanied him halfway across the state, taking the loneliness from his life and showing him a love he'd never imagined possible. His hotel rooms were more companionable, like a home of sorts, and she waited for him at the front of the stage while he performed. From his vantage point, his eyes always sought her out in the semi-dark. He felt calm and peaceful just knowing she was there.

He wrote prolifically, songs that both publicly and privately declared his love for her. The words surged into his head when he least expected: while driving the truck between gigs or in the dead of night when nothing stirred and Susan lay beside him, sleeping. There was a passion in his voice then, an intensity that often brought him perilously close to tears.

After a year, he gave up the road and they settled in Perth, where the night-time silence of the bush was replaced by the muted roar of traffic. He worked nights in a small bar. The wages were lousy, but he earned good tips. They bought a small cottage by the river and Susan hoped for a baby to make their relationship complete. But month after month he saw the hope die, to be replaced by a despondency in her eyes, her face.

'Never mind,' he reassured her. 'Relax. It'll happen when the time's right.'

He saw her look longingly at women pushing prams, or labouring behind bellies huge with child and knew he was powerless to comfort her. His words couldn't erase that awful need inside her. It ate away at her, at him, causing little niggles and fractures. *Why us?* he wanted to scream at the night sky, casting the question to the God he believed watched over them. *Why us?*

All Susan wanted was his child. At the time it seemed such a modest request.

One night, after his shift in the bar was over, a man came up and introduced himself. He was a manager, he said, of several local singers, and he liked what he'd seen and heard that night. 'You've got a certain style,' he said. 'And the songs are good. Who writes them?'

'I do.'

The man nodded. 'Very impressive. Perhaps you'd like to put together a demo tape. I might have some interested backers.'

The rest happened so quickly. Suddenly Declan was offered a generous recording contract. Pledges were made by executives in plush city offices. His future, and Susan's, looked promising

Then Susan was given the bad news and everything came crashing down.

His career was suddenly unimportant.

September, he thinks now, the word causing a shudder to run across his shoulders as he tries to push the memory back into the dark recesses of himself, and fails. It rises up inside, insistent, demanding he pay it proper attention. For too long he's kept it buried.

It was also September, three years after their marriage, when he laid her in the damp ground. It was a day of bleak rain and unseasonal cold, the chill wind echoing the aching misery in his heart. As suddenly as she'd come into his life, she'd gone – leaving a space too big to ever fill. After the graveside service was over and the few mourners had gone back to their warm homes, he'd sat on the ground next to her grave, unable to take himself from her side, beyond even tears.

Declan draws a deep breath, remembering, the pain still raw inside him after all this time. Susan: dark auburn hair and smiling mouth, freckles scattered across her nose. Breasts round and full, enough flesh to cup in his hands. It is five years since that rainy day, but God, he still misses her.

He'd taken to the road with his guitar again, after she'd died, walking away from the recording deal and the memories. The plans he'd made had been for Susan's future as much as his own, and they were no longer important. Instead, he'd found moderate success in small local halls in towns like this one: towns where the population was starved for music.

He stayed close to the coast at first, not venturing far inland. Then as the months – and years – passed, he travelled further out into the more remote areas. Back through the mining country he'd once visited with Susan – such as Tom Price and Wittenoom – and towns with Aboriginal names whose spelling ended in the letters 'ing' or 'up': Katanning. Gnowengerup. Manjinup. Koolyanobbing.

But the old songs he'd written for Susan had deserted him. Now he sang other people's words and music. Songs he'd heard on the radio. Songs that had no personal meaning. All the tunes he'd written for her, his wife, back in his happy days, he stored away, unable to bring himself to voice them again.

Now, though, between the gigs and the travelling he realises he can't escape the memories of her, though he's tried long and hard to. And he knows that one day he'll have to stop running. The anger and frustration still burn inside him, however. Anger at a God who'd taken the one person he loved, and frustration because he'd been unable to stop the cancer that had eaten away at her, reducing her to tired bones.

His last memory of her living slides towards him now: Susan lying on the hospital bed. Her skin is the same bleached colour of the sheets. Her hair is fanned out like a bloodied halo on the pillow.

'Hold me,' she whispers and in his mind's eye he threads his arms through the tangle of tubes that nourish her ravaged body and dull the pain. Through the coarse fabric of the hospital gown, he can feel her ribs all angular but tender to touch.

'Hold me,' she whispers again, her voice so faint that he wonders whether she has actually spoken or he has imagined the words, he is so tired from sitting beside her day and night, not daring to leave for any stretch of time in case the unspeakable happens. She raises her hand to his and he catches her fingers in his own. *Birdlike, fleshless*, he thinks, and his heart overflows, wishing that some miracle could let him take on her pain and spare her this agonising death.

'I am holding you,' he says.

He wonders if she can, in fact, feel his embrace and his voice sounds inordinately loud in that hospital room, bouncing off white sterile walls and reverberating back at him from what seems like a hundred different angles. He imagines his words sliding under the closed door that affords them a little privacy and floating down the hospital hallway, to be heard by everyone who passes.

'I love you. I need you,' he reassures her. 'Please don't give up. We can make it together, you and me. What about the children we'll have? All those little babies –'

And while he sits there, this last time, his arms wrapped carefully around her emaciated body, whispering his words of love and need and hope, the life ebbs from her. One long shudder, one drawn-out rasping breath and she lies still.

'Susan,' he whispers, his voice old as centuries. Then, '*Susan!*'

Dear Lord! He can't believe she's gone, isn't ready (will he ever be?) for her passing. Instead he wants to shake her, to judder the life back into her.

Consciously he wills her to breathe, draws back and searches her face for any sign of life. But her features have slackened and her eyes are closed. Commonsense tells him to lay her back on the bed and release her from his hold.

He sits for what seems like a long time, clasping her hand. Sobs shudder through his body as he watches her, his mind taking in a thousand single snapshot memories that will have to carry him through a lifetime. Eventually a nurse comes and unfolds his hand from hers. An orderly follows, lifting Susan easily onto a white-sheeted trolley, and takes her away. Away to the damp ground.

Now, remembering but not wanting to, Declan rolls over and buries his face in the pillow, pressing his grief back into that dark place inside. That was five years ago, and he's been travelling and running from the memories ever since. In that time he's seen the inside of too many dimly lit and acoustically bad local halls. There have also been too many bars, and hundreds of lonely motel rooms, as cramped as this room. He lets his eyes travel the walls and furniture and he wishes, not for the first time, that there had been a child during those three years he and Susan shared, some enduring reminder of their love, some continuation of her.

A scratching at the screen door catches his attention and he swings himself up onto the edge of the mattress, searching for the floor with his feet.

When he finally opens the door, a cat sits there, staring at him. It's grey, with yellow eyes and a scar on one ear.

'Hello,' he says, bending down to scratch the underside of its chin. The cat purrs loudly and winds itself around his legs. 'Where do you belong?'

As he says the words, he glances across at the building towards which the woman went earlier – Meg Halloran, she said her name was.

It's a square box-like house, similar to those in many of the country towns he's seen, with a verandah all around and the western side shaded by a stand of bonewood. As he watches, he sees her come around the corner of the building, a basket of washing balanced on her hip. She places the basket on the ground and starts to hang the wet garments on the line.

She moves, he thinks, like the cat, all languid and fluid and graceful. He can see the vague outline of her breasts as she extends herself towards the line, arms outstretched. Then she straightens up and, as though aware of his scrutiny, or maybe even his presence at the doorway, she glances in his direction.

Declan knows she cannot possibly see him through the netting on the screen door, yet he pulls back, positioning himself so he can no longer view her. And when he looks again, seconds later, she is gone, and all that is left to show she has ever been there is the washing slapping happily in the breeze.

CHAPTER 6

Dappled shade of bonewood

In all the fuss of Grady's leaving and Declan O'Brien's arrival, Meg has forgotten that Connie, Grady's sister, has planned a barbecue at her place this evening. Instead, her mind on other matters, she immerses herself in her book, stopping only to sip at the occasional glass of cold water and to make a sandwich for lunch. And it isn't until Connie arrives on Meg's doorstep, late afternoon, that Meg remembers.

'You *are* coming?' Connie chides her as they stand on the verandah in the dappled shade of the bonewood. 'You promised. And just because Grady's away –'

A cicada starts its chirrup in one of the nearby trees, then there's the slam of a door. Connie's words die away, unfinished, as Declan O'Brien walks from the room at the back of the service station over to his truck, which is parked in the shadows. He moves with an easy loping gait and

Connie, turning towards the sound of the door slamming, says, 'Who's that?'

'His name's Declan.'

'Declan?' She frowns. 'What sort of a name is Declan? And what's he doing here?'

'Firstly, I have no idea about his name,' Meg explains patiently, one part of her rising up against Connie's curiosity. For some inexplicable reason she feels a sense of proprietorship over the stranger who now walks across the yard. 'His truck's broken down, so he's waiting for Grady to come back and fix it. I said he could stay in the room down there. No one's using it.'

'Good sort, is he?' asks Connie, shielding her eyes with her hand and angling herself for a better look.

At thirty-seven, Connie is two years older than Meg. She's constantly lamenting the scarcity of local men, having decided more years ago than Meg can remember that she's destined to become a spinster. 'Who'd want me, anyway?' she often asks. 'I've been living by myself for too long now. Too independent, that's me. I'd drive a bloke crazy.'

Meg, studying her sister-in-law, silently agrees.

Connie, although not a woman of classical beauty with her wide soft mouth and dark eyes, possesses the kind of unusual prettiness that makes men stop and look twice. There's a sense of the gypsy about her, mysterious and exotic. She walks with a provocative swing of the hips and her hands move expressively as she speaks. But she has a way of tossing her head, swinging her hair back as she does, that gives the impression of indifference.

'It's her tongue,' Grady says, 'that drives men away. She's sarcastic and they don't know how to take her.'

Meg knows what Grady means; while Connie's eyes and mouth issue invitations, her words give off different signals.

Meg sometimes wants to take her aside and point this out, to give her a few tips on social etiquette. But she knows, too, that she could become the unwilling recipient of her sister-in-law's caustic tongue. So she's let the matter slide and she believes Connie's sudden interest in Declan O'Brien will be fleeting and perfunctory.

'A new man in town: that could prove interesting,' Connie says now, watching Meg closely. 'What's he doing out here, anyway?'

Meg shrugs. 'I have no idea.'

'You didn't ask?'

'No.' Meg suppresses a smile. Connie would have had no qualms in quizzing Declan O'Brien about his intentions. She names the town that Declan has already nominated as his destination. 'He's heading east, that's all I know.'

'Perhaps he's a travelling salesman?'

Meg shakes her head. 'I don't think so – at least I don't get that impression,' she adds hastily. 'He's got a guitar, though.'

'A guitar? Fancy that!'

Meg shrugs, dismissing the conversation. 'Well, I'll see you tonight, then.'

Connie makes to leave. She walks down the steps, away from Meg. 'Tonight,' she echoes. Then, at the last moment, before rounding the side of the house she calls, 'Why don't you invite your friend Declan to the barbecue?'

And before Meg can answer, she is gone from view.

After Connie leaves, Meg prepares a special salad. She's seen the recipe in a women's magazine and has been waiting for the right moment, namely Grady's absence, to test it. Grady likes his food plain, just as his mother used to prepare it. Meat and three veg. No fuss. No experimenting. Definitely nothing fancy.

Over the years there have been too many rejected meals, and mostly Meg has given up being creative in the kitchen. Now, she takes a piece of steak from the refrigerator and places it with the salad and a torch in a basket. Then she lets herself out the door.

It's almost dusk. The sun has completed its final descent over the wheat fields and is a red shimmering orb just above the western horizon. And although the intense heat of the day is fading, Meg can feel the remaining warmth of it still radiating from the bare ground as she stands in front of the verandah steps. Something – a noise, perhaps – makes her glance towards the room at the rear of the service station. Through the open window she can see the light of a single globe burning

Declan, she thinks, recalling his long, lean frame and wondering what his plans are for the evening. Perhaps he'll go to the pub for a meal, as she has suggested. By the look of him, he could do with a decent feed. He needs fattening up – that's what Grady, who is more than a few pounds overweight himself, would say.

Then she remembers the truck and the repairs needed, and wonders if he's short of money. On impulse she walks back inside the house and takes another piece of steak from the fridge.

She knocks on his door, wondering if she's doing the right thing, inviting him like Connie says. Perhaps he'd rather be by himself, not in the company of a woman and a strange one at that. There's the sound of movement from inside, then footsteps. He opens the door and stands there, his body silhouetted against the light.

'Hello,' he says, studying her.

Meg feels unnerved by his gaze, laid bare. She glances away, back into the interior of the room. The blue-and-white ticking on the mattress is creased, as though he has only just risen from it. The sheets are still folded on the table. His hair is rumpled and there's a surprised, sleepy look to his face, as though she's disturbed him.

'I'm sorry,' she stammers. 'I've woken you.'

'That's okay.' His face relaxes into a grin. 'I need to think about dinner, anyway.'

'That's what I've come about. There's a barbecue organised at Connie's. My sister-in-law,' she adds, by way of explanation. 'She lives down by the river. I've brought extra meat; I thought you might like to join us.'

Together they walk along the path at the edge of the paddock. The wheat is a shimmering mass in the sunset, all pink and silver and gold. Declan has relieved her of the picnic basket. He carries it effortlessly and she's aware of the sway of his body as he walks beside her, the way his arm almost touches hers.

It's only a few minutes to Connie's. The conversation is limited to the weather and the fact that the wheat is almost ready for harvesting. A cooler breeze has swung their way, coming from the river. Meg allows it to wash over her, just as she lets Declan's words wash over and around her.

She likes the sound of his voice. It flows and ebbs, and the words, once voiced, soar up to the already darkening sky. She's not really paying attention to them, more to the *sound* of them: the way they rise and fall, the intensity and feeling in them.

She stops at Connie's front gate and Declan opens it for her, swinging it forward with a flourish as he watches her steadily from under the brim of his hat.

'Do you ever take that thing off?' she asks with a tentative smile.

'What – the hat?' Her smile is mirrored in his eyes.

'Yes.'

'Sometimes.'

There is music and laughter coming from inside Connie's house and light spills onto the surrounding lawn from the open windows. Someone is singing, off-key. Meg walks along the path with Declan close behind.

'You don't wear it to bed, then?' she asks.

Why has she said that? And what will Declan think of her? Suddenly she dips her head at the audacity of her words, hoping the semi-dark hides the flush she can feel creeping along her cheeks.

One of Connie's friends comes to the door and saves her from the embarrassing moment. 'Come on through,' she says, waving them into the interior of the house, to the back verandah, which overlooks the water. 'Everyone's out there.'

CHAPTER 7

The country singer

Meg never ceases to be fascinated by Connie's small cottage by the river. The wallboards are painted blue. The verandah railings are a deep rust colour. Most of the rooms are filled with a motley assortment of furniture that Connie's collected over the years during the course of her travels. Sometimes Meg sees her leave for places unknown, her little car piled high with suitcases and canvasses, brushes and paints, and wishes she could clamber aboard, or that Connie would simply offer to take her. But an invitation has never been made.

Connie is a name short for Constance, Meg privately thinks is inappropriate for her sister-in-law. She's an artist, of sorts, and spends much of her time outdoors, painting earth and sky. She sells the results to a gallery in the city, where they are snapped up by overseas tourists for inordinately large sums of money. At the rear of her house, on a small rise overlooking the river, there's a studio where Connie can be found most daylight hours.

This is the studio that Meg and Declan walk to. Through the house and down the grassy slope they go, to a level area under a spreading gum. Connie is holding court there and several local men have gathered around her. One is strumming a guitar, but it sounds out of tune. Meg sees Declan wince, and remembers the instrument that he carried in from his truck, hours earlier. Perhaps she could have persuaded him to bring it tonight.

'Sorry,' she whispers. 'I didn't think we'd be being musical.'

For that one moment they are conspirators.

Connie glances up and sees them. 'Meg,' she calls, giving Declan an appraising look and waving her sister-in-law over. 'Come and introduce us.'

They walk across the grass, Meg aware of Connie's eyes on Declan. 'Well, well! What a surprise! Who do we have here?' Connie asks in a voice that doesn't sound surprised at all.

Meg introduces them. Connie shakes Declan's hand in the bush fashion, holding it, Meg privately thinks, a little too long. Connie is leaning in really close, staring into Declan's face. 'So, tell us a little about you,' she banters. 'Where have you been all my life?'

Connie's flirting; unashamedly making blatant sexual foreplay. Meg sees Declan hesitate and wonders if he will answer the question.

'I've been travelling,' he says simply at last.

'So,' Connie persists, either ignoring his reluctance or plain unaware of it. 'What do you *do*? For a job, I mean.'

'I'm a singer.'

The man next to Connie is still strumming his guitar. The sound of it grates at Meg, like flies buzzing at a closed window. Connie claps her hands together playfully like a child. 'I knew you could never be anything *ordinary!*' she exclaims, nodding sideways at the guitar. 'Tell me, do you play?'

'Yes.'

Meg suppresses a smile as the man slides his guitar under his chair. 'You don't say,' the man drawls. 'Maybe you could give us a tune later?'

Declan nods. 'Maybe.' He holds out his hand for the guitar. 'That sounds terrible,' he says. 'Here, let me.'

Someone hands them a drink and Meg finds herself sitting next to Declan on a rock at the edge of the river as he fiddles with the tuning pegs on the guitar. The river, at that point, is wide and the current strong. Meg knows from experience that if she tried to swim it, it would quickly carry her away.

She sits with him, she tells herself, more out of politeness than wanting to, feeling responsible for him being there. He strums the guitar, testing the pitch. The notes sounder truer now, more in tune. Declan eventually hands the guitar back.

A few others nod at them. The curious come up and introduce themselves with a handshake and the inevitable question, 'New in town, are you?'

'Just passing through. My truck's broken down.'

'Staying at the pub?'

'No, Meg here –' he pauses and glances in her direction, 'offered me a room at the back of the service station.'

It's fully dark now, the blackness stretching away infinitely behind them. Through it, Meg can hear the rush of the water. Someone lights a bonfire high on the riverbank. The darkness unfolds around them. Flames light up the surrounding trees and send shadows darting out into the night.

Everyone has brought food. Steak and sausages for the barbecue. Salads. Cake for after.

'I've come empty-handed,' Declan says, surveying the fire and grimacing. As he talks, the firelight is reflected in his face, his eyes.

Finally they eat, and the silences between words are comfortable. Meg finds herself telling him a little of her life, about Grady and how they've been married for fifteen years.

'You must have been very young,' Declan says.

'A child bride, almost. I was twenty. Old enough to know better, but too young to resist.'

He gives her a curious look.

'And you?' she asks. 'Are you married?'

'I was once,' he says tersely and turns his head away.

Meg can see a tightening of his mouth. Obviously the subject is a raw one.

Instead, he tells her about his job and how he stays on the road. 'It's a funny life – odd, I suppose to some, but I like it. The not putting down roots, the ability to pack up and move on when the mood takes you, the being spontaneous and flexible and free: I kind of like that.'

'What's the longest you've ever stayed in one place?'

'Just over two years. And you?'

Meg nods to the west. 'We came from further out, my dad and I, years ago, and I've scarcely left. Not for more than a few days, anyway, and that was only to go down the road a bit.' She names the town Declan is heading to in a few days time. 'I suppose this'll be where they bury me.'

'You've never been to the city?' he asks and frowns.

She shakes her head.

'How come?'

She shrugs. 'It just never happened. Grady always promised we would, then after we were married we never seemed to have the time. He's always busy.'

'So you never have holidays?'

'No.'

'*You* could have gone, though.'

'By myself?'

'Yes.'

'I suppose.'

She glances away on an intake of breath, her attention not really on the scene before her. She's thinking that Grady promised her they'd travel after the wedding, but he's always ready with some excuse or other. There's too much work, or not enough money. But deep down she knows Grady has never had any intention of taking her. It has all been a sham, a pretence, a ploy.

'Marry me,' he'd said and she'd agreed, thinking that her life was somehow going to be transformed.

How could she have been so naïve?

Declan stares around him at the townsfolk who have gathered on the banks of the river. They seem a kindly lot, honest country folk like those he has met in similar towns. No pretensions. No facades. They just say things as they are, not as they might be.

There's Horace from the general store, the one who gave him directions to Meg Halloran's earlier in the day, and the woman from the local post office. The chap with the guitar is looking daggers at him (he didn't mean to embarrass the man). Connie, Meg's sister-in-law, is laughing, dancing up to him in the glow of the fire, her eyes shining. She's making a not-so-subtle play for him, asking questions and trying to dig into his inner core. Why do women do that?

For one brief moment Declan wonders what it would be like to put down roots in a place like this, to stop the wandering. And what exactly, he asks himself, is he searching for? A sense of family, of belonging? Of walking to the store and knowing the name of every person he passes and the names of their children and dogs; not just nodding politely to strangers in the street?

Susan, he recalls abruptly — that's what he's been searching for.

In his mind he tries to invoke the much-loved essence of her, a fragment of memory, however small. But it's ephemeral, like the wind, and it dances away from him, skulking in the shadows beyond the trees.

Susan would have loved it here, he considers now. The sense of community, the fun. The interweaving of lives. Even Connie's precociousness and Meg's reticence, that subtle feeling of sadness that seeps from deep inside her. Susan would have sat and watched and taken it all in, and then they would have discussed it all later, tossed observations to each other as they lay together in bed, arms and hands and legs entwined.

But Susan is long gone.

He glances across the river, to the place where the land is cleared and the wheat fields begin again. A reflection from the flames dances there, merging with the moonless black of the night. Declan feels the wind against his face and knows he'd be constrained, suffocated, by this life. There is something to be said about the travelling, always moving on. He can hide his pain in a kaleidoscope of settings and melt into crowds in strange places, to find the anonymity he craves.

Meg is talking and he watches her mouth move as she does. She's pretty enough, he acknowledges, in the usual way, but he's often surrounded by pretty women, especially in the big towns. Invariably they come up to him after a gig, asking for his autograph or pushing a piece of paper at him bearing their phone number. But he seldom encourages them, rarely calls. They mean nothing and he'll be gone, come morning. There is no point, really.

He thinks about long nights in other lonely beds, strange towns and motel rooms. Street lights slanting through open windows and the frenzied barking of dogs. Occasionally he has woken next to a woman, a stranger, pale early-morning light flooding the room. And for one awful shameful moment he's failed to remember her name, or how he met her, or even how he'd come to be in her bed. All he knows is that the woman isn't Susan and, making some excuse, he'd let himself out into that bright dawn light and driven away, heading towards yet another town.

Pretty women, he thinks, remembering and still watching Meg as she leans forward, her hair falling across her face like a veil, obscuring her features for a moment. She's intelligent, he senses that, just as he suspects that passions run strong within her, though as yet he's unsure what those passions are, or even whether she recognises them herself.

Compared with a lot of country women, she has a softness and calmness that he finds reassuring. And like him, she can, he suspects, be a deep thinker who can be moved by words or music.

The light from the fire is reflected on her face, and the fabric of her dress pushes against her breasts. She looks fleetingly towards him and in that brief moment, as though aware of his scrutiny or his thoughts, glances quickly away. He feels an ache deep in his groin.

She stares ahead for what seems like a long time and he searches to find something, anything, to fill the space between them. He feels he has encroached upon her in an odd inexplicable way. She's married, after all, to the absent Grady. He has no right to these thoughts.

Just when he thinks it might be prudent to walk away and use the excuse of having to fetch another drink, she turns to face him, her expression earnest. 'Do you like to read?' she asks.

He nods and stretches his long legs in front of him, relieved, one part of him loath to walk away, ever. 'Books? Yes. And you?'

'Oh, novels, poetry, whatever. When I get the opportunity.'

'The time, you mean?'

The question hangs between them. 'Not exactly,' she replies guardedly.

Silence again, but this time he waits for her to fill it. Then, when he sees that she won't, he throws the idea at her, studying her face as his words fall. 'I used to write most of my own songs.'

'The tunes?'

He nods and goes on. 'Not just the music, but the words as well.'

'Oh.' Suddenly she seems interested.

'Words need to be sung,' he goes on. 'They need to have melody and rhythm and voice. They need to move you, to make you laugh or cry.'

'You write sad songs?'

'And happy. Happiness can move you to tears just as much as sadness.'

She looks pensive. 'I suppose so.' Then, 'You said you *used* to write songs. You don't do that any more?'

'*No.*' The word comes out harsh and fast.

'Why not?'

Declan shrugs. Part of him wants to blurt out the reason, that the creativity seems to have deserted him since Susan's death, or that the songs only remind him of her and the monstrous loss he's suffered.

'Why don't you play the guitar for us?' Meg suggests, defusing the situation, as though realising his discomfort.

He dismisses the idea. 'Oh, you don't want to listen to me.'

'Of course we do,' says Connie, suddenly coming up behind them, like a playful ghost from the dark. For a fraction of a second she rests her hand on Declan's shoulder. 'We need something to liven us up.'

Later they walk back to the service station in the dark. Meg carries the empty picnic basket. Declan holds the torch. The light beam quivers and dances before them, emphasising the unevenness of the ground.

'Careful,' he says, guiding her around a large pothole.

The pressure of his hand sends what seems like a series of small electric shocks along her arm, and she flinches away from his touch. 'Don't,' she wants to say. 'Please don't touch me. It reminds me of all the pleasurable things that are missing in my life.'

But of course she says nothing; simply lowers her head and places one foot in front of the other.

At the doorway to his room, the cat rubs against Declan's legs, purring loudly. 'She likes you,' says Meg, waiting while he steps inside. 'Usually she runs a mile at any sign of strangers.'

'The cat has taste.' He smiles as he clicks off the torch. Meg looks at it blankly, her mind only half paying attention to what he is saying. 'I was only joking,' he adds.

'Joking?' She swings her head up.

'About the cat having taste. It was just a joke.'

'Oh.'

She looks at his guitar lying on the table and imagines his hands fingering the strings. Then her eyes slide sideways, studying those same hands. 'How long have you been playing?' she asks.

Declan thinks for a moment. 'Most of my life, I suppose. I was just a little tyke when I began. Three or four, perhaps. My father used to play and I picked it up from him.'

'You never had lessons?'

'No.'

'You're very good.'

'Thanks.'

Meg is still standing in the doorway. She thinks there's awkwardness between them, a stilted politeness. She nods to the interior of the room, her eyes taking in the bed and dresser, the old table and two chairs, as though she is seeing them for the first time. 'Grady and I lived here when we were first married.'

'In this one room?'

'Yes, for about six months, until we built the house.'

'Must have been kind of cramped, for two.'

Meg lowers her eyes, unable to meet his. Momentarily embarrassed, she twists the wedding ring on her finger. Round and round it goes, smooth under her hand. 'Oh, you know. We were newly married and closeness wasn't something we wanted to avoid.'

She thinks about those early days with Grady, the way he waltzed her around the room the first night they spent together and they collapsed laughing onto the bed. She remembers how his hands and body explored hers, tentatively, clumsily, for they were both inexperienced. And last, but not least, she remembers how her life has altered and realigned itself over the years, so much so that she can't wait for Grady's absences, and she acknowledges that the closeness she once felt to her husband has faded to indifference.

'And now?' asks Declan

She glances away, biting her lip, unable to answer him. 'Well, then,' she says, turning towards the door. 'Sleep tight.'

Back in the house, Meg lies in her bed in the dark. Sleep eludes her. Instead she thinks about what Declan said earlier in the evening, his surprise that she'd never been to the city and the bit about leaving by herself.

She imagines boarding the train that passes through twice a week, sitting on the seat and staring out the windows as the township moves from her view, disappearing into the wish-wash green of trees and wheat and distant horizon. But she has always been too afraid to do it. She acknowledges the thought and the reason she has never gone.

'Because,' she whispers now, 'if I leave I'll never come back.'

Declan replays the scene, earlier in the day, when Meg lifts the sheets from the cupboard and sets them on the bed. The plump fullness of her upper arms is visible in the sleeveless dress. Her breasts, as she bends down, strain against the fabric. Capable arms, he thinks.

Then she offers to make the bed.

He's been making his own bed for years, unaided, and some part of him feels humiliated by the suggestion. Is she insinuating that he can't do it himself, or that she thinks it's her job? He doesn't know and feels reluctant to ask, for fear of offending her.

'Thanks, but I'll be fine,' he says, waving her away.

Is it disappointment he sees on her face?

Now he's certain he won't sleep a wink in this strange bed in this strange room. As she walks away to the house just now he watches every step she takes. Through the square of light that spills out of his open doorway onto the uneven ground beyond, she goes, then into the darkness where she merges quickly into the night. Only the beam of the torchlight indicates her progress.

Some part of him wants to reach out and pull her back, to tell her that she shouldn't have demeaned herself by offering to make his bed earlier in the day. Then, with clever words, he wants to wipe the sadness from her eyes and make her laugh.

He's not certain how long he stands there, after he sees the house lights go on and watches her shadow move across what must be the bedroom window. Possibly it's only minutes, though maybe longer. But one by one the lights go out again and all is dark.

There's no sound, except for the call of a night bird. The breeze stirs and caresses his face, and he thinks again of Susan and her smile, and the way she'd had of loving him. And that ache of grief begins again. It's still there, deep in his belly.

CHAPTER 8

Sounds of the sea

Somehow the following day seems different from all the others. As Meg goes about her chores, her heart is light and a song dances on her tongue. Excitement bubbles away inexplicably inside her.

From time to time she goes to the front door, on some pretext or other, and looks out to the room at the rear of the service station. She's hoping to catch sight of Declan. But, despite the heat, the door remains shut and except for his truck parked in the dappled shade, there is nothing to remind her that he even exists.

Perhaps she has dreamt him. She can barely see the truck; the glare is so bright and it is so dark in under the trees. Then she laughs at her own silliness. Of course Declan is real. Didn't he walk with her to Connie's place last night? Didn't he sit under that spreading gum after the meal was finished and tease music from his guitar that made her want to weep?

Eventually she walks across the paddock to the service station. It is ten o'clock. In one hand she carries a jug of milk, which she is using as an excuse for the visit; in the other she holds a loaf of bread fresh from her oven. Perhaps Declan will want some for his breakfast.

Meg knocks once on the closed door. There is no sound. She knocks harder.

'Come in,' a voice calls.

Tentatively she opens the door. Declan is sitting at the table, a notebook in front of him and a pen in his hand. He turns to her with a frown.

'Sorry,' she says, immediately regretting her intrusion. She should have stayed away, left him to his own devices. It is her curiosity that has brought her here.

'That's okay,' he says, laying down his pen. A sheepish smile plays around the corners of his mouth. 'I had the urge to write; that's all. And when I do, nothing else matters. Time disappears.'

Meg studies his features, again liking what she sees. His is an honest face, square and clean-cut, with a strong jaw line and high cheekbones. A shaft of sunlight streams through the window and falls untidily on the table where he sits. Dust motes dance in its brilliance, weaving and bobbing on a current of warm air. He puts the cap on the pen and places it on the table in front of him, stretches his arms out, testing muscles.

She's still holding the milk and the bread. Now, remembering them and the reason for her visit, she holds them out to him. 'I brought you something for your breakfast,' she says.

He scrapes the chair back and walks over to her, the air moving around him as he sweeps the dust motes in his wake. His hand touches hers as he takes her offering. It is momentary and fleeting, the touch, and she pulls her hand back with a jerk.

Her fingers are shaking – why does he have this effect on her? – and she folds her arms across her chest, tucking her fingers between the sides of her breasts and her upper arms. She pauses there, unsure of what to say or do, and stares at the angry purple mass of clouds along the horizon.

Declan quotes some lines about the sense of space and distance in the land, his mouth close to her ear.

Without her realising it, he has come up beside her and the nearness of his voice causes Meg to jerk away again. She presses her lips together, her mind searching, scrambling, for the origin of the poem. Who wrote it?

'Slessor?' she says at last, the words stirring a vague familiarity.

Declan nods. 'It's "South Country": one of my favourites. Let's see if I can remember the rest.'

He stares past her and she wonders yet again why he compels her so, this stranger who drove in from the bush less than a day ago. Her heart is pounding and the palms of her hands are damp. She is holding her breath, she realises, and she forces herself to breathe slowly, pushing the air silently from her lungs.

Poetry. She is stunned. *He's quoting me poetry.*

Her mind immediately skips to the kitchen drawer and the old exercise book tucked away with her recipe books, a place where Grady will never find it. She has her own collection of scribblings there, some of which she's made up herself; others she's seen and read in books and has dutifully copied down. She's never told Grady or Connie before, or anyone else for that matter. Connie wouldn't understand and Grady would laugh at her if he knew. But Declan never would, she is sure of that. Isn't he a composer of words, after all, with his song writing?

Declan stops and looks at her thoughtfully. She suffers his scrutiny for a moment, then glances away. She really doesn't understand this man, or her interest in him. Why does he fascinate her? What is it about him that compels her attention? The possibilities jumble in her mind, confusing her.

Puzzled, she turns to face him again. He's no longer looking at her, but at the purple mass of clouds, a surprised expression on his face.

'Do you think it's going to rain?' he asks softly.

Meg considers the question before glancing out at the sky again. 'It might,' she answers. 'Then, again, it might not. Grady would say it's something to do with the shape of the clouds and the way they sit, either high or low in the sky.'

'And what does Meg Halloran say?'

'Oh,' she says, 'it's all in the wind. You can smell the rain coming for miles around here. There's a sweet sickly tang to the air. It comes from the gidgee tree. Have you ever smelt it?' Then she laughs as she realises that Declan is from the country too. 'Forget that. Of course you have.'

He places the milk and bread on the table and reaches for his cigarettes. He takes two from the packet and offers her one. 'Smoke?'

She nods and takes it between her fingers. 'Thanks.'

He holds the match out to her and she takes a deep puff, watching the smoke unfurl as the paper catches. Grady hates it when she smokes, so she doesn't, mostly. He can smell it on her breath, he says as he curls his lip in disgust – even though Meg wonders at the accuracy of his sense of smell, or the overall importance of his observations, seeing he rarely comes near her these days.

Now that first breath of tobacco smoke, the acrid rawness of it, catches in her throat and she resists the sudden urge to cough. Instead she takes another puff, fighting the sensation, and leans back against the doorframe. From the corner of her eye she sees Declan raise his cigarette to his mouth.

'So,' he says, fixing her with a deep look. 'What's it like living in this place?'

'It's okay, I suppose. I guess as bush towns go, it's much the same as any other.'

He nods and flicks the ash away. 'So what do you do?'

'To keep busy?' She thinks for a moment, searching her mind for an answer. 'Me? Oh, goodness. Nothing as exciting as you. I just keep things going about this place – you know, cooking and cleaning – and I do Grady's books.'

'No.' He shakes his head. 'I mean, what do you *do*? For yourself. For *Meg*.'

She glances down at her hands and straightens her fingers either side of the cigarette, splaying them out against her belly. 'Sometimes,' she says softly, avoiding his gaze and staring through the doorway at some point beyond his line of vision. 'Sometimes I write poetry.'

She presses her lips together and looks directly at him.

'Poetry?'

'Yes.'

'Can I read some?' he asks.

She shakes her head. 'No,' she says hesitantly. 'I don't think so. Anyway, I've never shown the poems to anyone before. I'm sure they're not very good and I wouldn't want you to laugh.'

'I wouldn't laugh.'

He says it so earnestly, so reassuringly, that she almost changes her mind. A few minutes, that's all it will take to run to her kitchen and bring the book back. No, she thinks, suddenly shy. There's a lot of herself and her own emotions in those poems. Letting Declan read them would be like standing naked before him.

She pushes herself upright, away from the doorframe and takes a nervous draw on the cigarette. 'Forget it,' she says abruptly. 'I shouldn't have told you.'

'Why not?'

She shrugs. 'Sometimes it seems silly, that's all. Writing poetry.'

'No sillier than writing songs.'

'At least you get to sing your songs.'

'And your poems – don't you ever read them aloud to anyone?'

'Like who? Around here, the people are mostly simple country folk. They'd think I was mad if I started reciting poetry.'

'Tell me,' he says fiercely. 'What are your dreams, Meg Halloran?'

She throws her head back and laughs. 'Dreams?' she says, biting her bottom lip. 'I don't have *dreams!* How could I, living here?'

'You have to dream, to have goals, things you want in life, from life. What *do* you want from life, Meg?' He prompts her. 'Children? Happiness? Love?'

'We all want those,' she replies quietly.

She wonders why she feels ridiculously like crying. What does he mean by firing these questions at her? And why does he tease emotions from her that she's kept hidden for so long?

Children, he said.

Her mind slides sideways to the babies she's lost. How many? She'd rather forget. Only one went full term and he was buried in the small local cemetery. She goes there every week to lay flowers against the gravestone, then she sits for a while and thinks about how different life might have been had he lived. The others were mere months or weeks old when they cramped from her body, unformed, yet they were hers just the same and she grieved for them all equally. A deep gut-wrenching, hollow kind of grief that she feels, even now.

'You have to have dreams, Meg,' he goes on, bringing her back to the present. 'And you have to keep those dreams alive somehow. If you don't, then life's a slow path to death, I reckon.'

'There's a poem about dreams I remember,' she offers, a memory stirring inside her.

He stops and stubs out the last of the cigarette in the ashtray on the table, then looks directly at her. 'Tell me.'

'If you can dream – and not make dreams your master. If you can think – and not make thoughts your aim,' she says, the words jerking back to her from somewhere in her hazy past.

'If you can meet with Triumph and Disaster,' he breaks in quietly, *'and treat those two impostors just the same.'*

'Kipling,' she whispers, feeling a lurch deep in her belly.

The words are now as familiar to her as the wind, the sun and the moon. As familiar as the paddocks of wheat that stretch away towards the horizon. As familiar as –

Declan, she realises suddenly. *The words are as familiar as Declan*.

The floodgates have opened inside her. She needs to tell her story – well, parts of it, anyway. It all comes rushing out and she stumbles over the words in an effort to be heard. Hesitating at first, then firm and clear, she unfolds most of it. Things she's hardly admitted to herself and never told anyone else, even Grady.

She recalls the way, as a girl, she dreamt of the city and smaller confined spaces, of losing herself there among the streets and traffic and wall-to-wall housing she'd seen in photographs in magazines. She remembers, feelings wakening inside her that she'd long-since thought dead, how she dreamed of an education and a job where someone paid her at the end of every week. A job that made her feel important and worthwhile and not just an appendage of her husband. A job that let her think and make decisions and feel important. Not this monotonous daily grind that simply builds boredom and resentment.

'I have to ask Grady for money,' she says. 'Not that he minds, but *I* do. It's demeaning. There are times when I want to be independent so badly. I want to be able to support myself and not have to be reliant on anyone.'

'You could be, if you really wanted to.'

She shrugs. 'I don't have the skills. When I was younger I wanted to travel and explore and –' Her voice trails away and she puffs on the cigarette. 'Anyway, it's too late now.'

'It's never too late.'

She pauses, considering for a moment before she shares her one special secret dream. 'I – '

For a moment she's unable to continue. She's aware that she is perilously close to tears, so she blinks them away, swallows hard, perplexed about the reason this confidentiality should suddenly move her so.

'I've always wanted to see the sea,' she continues in a determined yet wavering voice.

'Why haven't you?'

She thinks about the question and finds no valid reason. 'I don't know.' She shrugs. 'Grady promised to take me after we were married, but we never seemed to have the time or the money.'

'Does he know how badly you want to go?'

She shakes her head, not trusting herself to speak. And when she does, her voice is so quiet that she wonders if he can hear. 'Tell me, what's it like?'

'The sea?'

'Yes.'

He's obviously thinking; she can tell by the way he furrows his brow and narrows his eyes. He looks upwards, to the left, as though remembering images and scenes. A fleeting look of sadness crosses his face and then it's gone. He smiles at her. 'Ah, the sea.'

'Yes.' She leans forward, waiting.

'The sea can be wild at the height of a storm, waves crashing and tearing at the sand until they drag it all away, and you can hardly see in front of you for the salt spray and wind. Yet on a calm day the water runs up the sand, all gentle-like, then it slides away. On and on it goes, and it's real nice to lie there in the sun, with your eyes closed, listening to the sounds.'

'The sounds?'

'Gulls flying overhead. The lap, lap of water. Then other times it's so quiet you can almost hear your own heartbeat.'

She listens to his words, conjuring up her own images. They sparkle in the imagined sunlight. They dance off waves. They roll and surge until she can almost smell the salt tang and hear the sound of gulls crying.

Meg sighs and closes her eyes against the images. One day, she promises. One day she'll go and see for herself.

CHAPTER 9

Seams of conflict

2005
The wheat fields, Western Australia

'That's the way your mother told it to me, anyway,' says Aunt Connie. She sinks back against the pillows on her hospital bed, looking much older than her seventy-two years.

She seems tired. There are blue-black smudges under her eyes, and her skin has a papery translucent appearance. Outside night is falling and through the window I can see a flock of birds winging across a darkening, almost indigo sky. 'Gemma, if you don't mind, dear,' she adds, closing her eyes, 'we might leave it there for today. I need to rest.'

The retelling of the story seems to have taken a toll on her, that is physical as well as mental. I can see the way the muscles in her face move as she speaks, the way her hands clench, then unfold. She's been working the memories, recalling conversations and actions that took place before I was born or even conceived.

Sitting beside her, I wait and let the story she's begun to tell me sink into my consciousness. I know Connie's barely scratched the surface of her tale and the impatient part of me wants to know the rest immediately. 'Keep going,' I want to say to her. 'Tell me what happened next.'

But I can see, by the steady rise and fall of her chest, that my aunt is asleep.

I let myself out of the room and walk down the hospital corridor, the heels of my shoes clicking on the tiles as I go. A nurse nods to me as I pass. 'Sleeping, is she?' she asks.

'Yes.'

'Well, goodnight, then.'

I step into the night and the air, still warm, wraps itself around me. Through the streets I go, heading to the place my parents called home: this tiny fibro cottage with a verandah all around.

The telephone is ringing as I let myself in the front door. It's Greg. 'Hi,' he says and I close my eyes against the sound of his voice. Inexplicably I feel like crying.

'Hi, yourself,' I say, suddenly exhausted.

'Gem,' he goes on. 'I want to come for the funeral. It's not right, my not being there to support you.'

Part of me desperately wants him to come, and the other tells me to stop him. 'You barely knew my father,' I say, 'and it's a long way to travel.'

'But I want to be there for you,' he assures me.

Tears well up in my eyes and I fight them back. Greg's so selfless, always considering others before himself. Why can't I be like that?

'I love you, Gem,' he says, and his voice sounds sad, so sad. Then, 'What's happening to us?'

'What do you mean?'

'I'm losing you.'

I consider the statement for a moment.

'Gem, are you still there?'

'Yes.'

We say goodnight, the issue of his coming still unresolved. I shower and slide into bed, my *old* bed that I slept in as a child, in that bright pink room. It feels small and cold, and lonely.

I lie there, thinking of the conversation we've just had and the underlying seams of conflict in our lives.

'What's happening to us?' he said. 'I'm losing you.'

Is he? I don't know and I'm too damn tired, too exhausted, to think. My thoughts keep turning back to my mother and the stranger named Declan, the man who quoted her poetry and told her of other, more exciting lives.

Sleep descends, a grey blanket, caught up somehow in Aunt Connie's story. And when I wake it's a new day, warm already, and the birds are calling endlessly from the paddocks beyond.

CHAPTER 10

One defining moment of truth

'The sea,' says Meg. 'Tell me, what's it like?'

Then, without warning, the memory comes rushing back. Declan closes his eyes, trying to push it away, but it's strong, so strong, and begs to be acknowledged.

It was the last time he'd taken Susan there, a month before she died. He didn't accept it then, hadn't really admitted to himself that there were so few days left in her life. In fact he'd almost convinced himself that the doctor's prognosis was wrong. She'd looked so well that past week that this monstrous thing called cancer eating away insidiously at her body couldn't possibly be happening to Susan – *his Susan*. Somehow she'd get well and life would go on the same. It was all a terrible mistake.

In hindsight, he hadn't truthfully been able to consider the alternatives.

Susan seemed unusually frail that day, and pale. Her skin was almost translucent, her eyes huge and dark in her face. The bones at the base of her neck protruded sharply, as though the flesh had fallen away from her body there.

A stiff breeze blew and the hem of her dress whipped around her bare calves. She'd let go of his hand and bent to pull it down – to hide the thinness of her legs, he supposed. Then she'd folded her arms across her chest, putting up a barrier of sorts between them. The pulling away: was she trying to prepare him in some way, he wonders now, to train him for the eventuality of her not being there?

The sand was damp between their toes and, as they reached the rock ledge at the end of the bay, a flock of gulls had risen in one screaming mass, protesting at the human intrusion. Susan had laughed and reached down for a shell that lay exposed on the sand.

'Oh, look!' she'd cried, turning it over to see the inside. 'Mother-of-pearl. How beautiful.' Then, 'What a shame it had to die.'

She'd been breathing hard, too hard he remembers now, for so little exertion. Her face had a haunted fearful look and when she offered him the shell to look at, her hand had trembled. He'd closed his own hand over it, wanting to reassure her that everything would be all right, that somehow she'd – *they'd* – get through this. But she'd looked away, not meeting his gaze as she usually did.

It was at that precise moment that the undeniable reality had hit him – in one defining moment of truth: the finality of her disease. He knew with awful certainty that their days together were precious and numbered. And, more importantly, he knew that she knew too.

Declan closes his eyes against the memory and hauls his mind back to the present. He has an urgent need to remove himself from this dingy room at the rear of Grady Halloran's service station – which feels claustrophobic and vaguely threatening – and move freely in all the space outside.

He needs to breathe fresh air and feel the sun on his face, needs the wind to ruffle his hair and sweep through the dark inner part of him that he's been trying to lose for longer than he cares to remember. Yet he doesn't want to distance himself from this woman. He wants her comforting presence and the soothing tone of her voice. She reminds him that he's still alive, although some days it doesn't seem so, and that he still has needs and desires.

'Do you want to go for a walk?' he asks abruptly.

They make their way down to the river, along the same path they took last night. The land looks different in the sunlight: brighter, less forgiving. He walks quickly. She strides along beside him and, although he's aware she's struggling to keep up, he continues at that speed until the service station is left well behind and he can see the glint of water through the trees. Only then does he slow his pace.

They walk in silence. At first he's unsure what to say to her. The thoughts jam in his mind, presenting themselves as a confused jumble. Where to start? he wonders, knowing for certain that if he doesn't release them they'll consume him in some monstrous way.

When they reach the riverbank he stops and rests his back against an old gum. He can feel the bark digging into his back through his shirt, but he doesn't care. The feeling is nothing compared with long-ago hurts. In fact it grounds him and makes everything seem real. He wants the day to go on forever. Here, beside the river, the past is far removed from his life now.

So why can't he let it go?

He stares up towards a sky so blue it almost makes his eyes ache. A lone crow calls, the sound harsh, and he flinches away from it. In the distance he can hear the melody of other birds. The sun beats down, baking the hard earth. Meg wipes a hand across her forehead where beads of perspiration have gathered.

'Come on,' he says. 'Let's go a bit further down.'

He moves away from the tree and walks along the hard bony ridge of the bank towards the three silos silhouetted against the sky. He blinks at the glare from their surface and lets his eyes adjust. The town sprawls there, though he doesn't intend to walk that far. He needs solitude and space, not intrusion. Meg follows.

They walk underneath the gums that overhang the water, stepping between the dappled puddles of shade. It's dark under the trees, the breeze there like liquid.

He glances at her from time to time, but she's looking steadfastly ahead, carefully stepping over loose rocks. Once she holds his gaze then looks away, a disconcerted look on her face.

What are we doing? her expression says. *Where are we going?*

He stops at the water's edge, bending for a moment to let his fingers trail across its surface. The water is surprisingly cold and he rubs his hands together. 'I need to talk,' he says and his voice floats upwards until it merges with the blue of the sky.

At last his own story comes tumbling out. He tells her about Susan, the way they met and about their brief life together, how she died. He details those last days she spent in the hospital and how he felt as he finally walked away alone.

As he speaks, in his mind he hears his footfalls along those lonely hospital corridors. He recalls how quiet the house was that first night, how he woke constantly, feeling for her in the bed beside him, and how the wracking sobs that followed left his throat raw and aching.

His voice sounds like a stranger's, the words not his. The tone is hard, flinty. He tries to dampen the emotion creeping into it as he tells her of his pain and his belief for a long time afterwards that he couldn't bear to go on living. He tells her that he eventually sold the city house and went back on the road, but that he was unable to sing the old songs.

'There was too much sadness there,' he says. 'The songs brought it all back, so I had to find new ones that had no memories attached.'

Finally he tells her that he's closed himself off emotionally and not allowed himself to get too close to any woman in the intervening years. 'The opportunity's been there,' he admits, 'but I couldn't bear the hurt again.'

'So you won't even allow yourself the possibility?'

He shakes his head. They are picking their way along the edge of the river and he looks down into its muddy depths. The water swirls away, endlessly, pulling leaves, brown and soggy, in its wake. Susan's face, or the one he remembers, looms in his mind and is gone.

'I don't think I can.'

'You never had children, then?'

'No.'

He changes the subject, turning it back to her. 'And you?' he asks.

She closes her eyes. 'That's probably never meant to be.' Her voice softens as she speaks and he hears an immeasurable sadness there. Her eyes, when she opens them, are bright with unshed tears.

'I'm sorry,' he says. 'I didn't mean to upset you.'

She shakes her head and doesn't speak.

'I *have* upset you.'

Further along there's a woman standing on the bank, wearing a wide-brimmed straw hat and holding a fishing rod.

'There's Connie,' says Meg, coming to a halt. The woman looks in their direction and, seeing them, waves.

It's obvious, by the way she's standing, that Meg wants to go no further. And Declan knows that to meet up with Connie will spoil what has just passed between them, this sharing of confidences.

'We'd better be going back, then,' he offers and Meg nods in agreement.

It isn't until they are almost at the place where they must leave the river and walk back up the track to Meg's home, that Declan finds the gemstone.

It is lying exposed on the grass in the shade and he almost doesn't see it, so dark are the striations. He picks it up and it lies snugly in the palm of his hand. The bands – three in total, slightly darker than the base colour – are concentric like the rings of a tree trunk. The colours are faded, as though they've been leached out, so he bends down and dips it in the water. Immediately the stone assumes rich warm hues, the colours of the earth: russet and coffee and amber.

He hands it to her. 'Here,' he says, 'this is for you.'

Immediately he's startled by his own impetuousness. Since Susan, he's given not one thing to anyone, so why now? Granted, the stone has cost him nothing, but its sheer natural beauty is worth more than anything money could buy.

'I think its agate. *Chalecedony quartz*. At least, that type of stone usually has coloured bands like that.'

For one seemingly endless moment Meg hesitates, and he thinks she may refuse it. *Take it, it's a gift*, he begs silently. Then she smiles and reaches out.

'Thank you. It's beautiful.' She turns it over, inspecting the bands. 'It must be very old.'

He shrugs. 'Thousands of years, probably. In ancient times agate was said to quench thirst and protect from fevers. Magicians in Persia used it to divert storms.'

'You're very knowledgeable.'

'Mmm.' He matches her smile. 'And most of it useless. Well,' he adds, trying to defuse the awkwardness of the situation, 'I guess we'd better be going back then.'

They walk back to her house in silence. Meg holds the rock, lifting it up to look at it from time to time. She examines it more, he suspects, because she doesn't know what to say to him, than because she is curious. When they reach the bottom of her steps, she asks him in for a drink.

'Tea, coffee or cold: the choice is yours,' she offers.

Inside, he sits at the laminex-topped table and waits as she fills the jug. Then she reaches up and opens an overhead cupboard, removes two cups and sits them on the bench. He's strongly aware of the swell of her breasts against her blouse as she moves, and the way her hair falls loosely about her shoulders.

Something rises up inside him, acute and strong, a mixture of grief and desire rolling away from him in an untidy blur. He wonders what it might feel like to run his finger the length of her neck, or to hold her dark hair in his hands. How would it feel to have her beneath him, to raise his body in unison with hers, to kiss her mouth and her breast and belly? The desire is, in itself, a surprise. It has been such a long, long time since he has felt like this about anyone.

He feels himself harden at the thought and glances away, avoiding her gaze as she turns back towards him. How long, he wonders, since he has felt like this? He studies instead the row of canisters on the bench, trying to distract himself. There are five in total, cream with green embossed lettering. Coffee. Tea. Rice. Sugar. Flour.

She takes the one marked Coffee and ladles two teaspoons into the cups. Then she rummages in one of the kitchen drawers, taking something out and placing it on the table in front of him.

It's a tattered exercise book, and he knows instantly why. Since she told him about the poems she's written, he's had the sense that she'll eventually fetch them and let him read them. He wants to badly; to see the words she's put down, the way she's joined them and the rhythm they make. Some inner part of him wants – no, *needs* – to know more about her. And what better way than through her writing?

He moves to open the book, but she stops him with her hand. 'Not here. Not now,' she says. 'Take them to your room and read them whenever. Just promise me one thing.'

'Yes.'

'That you'll never tell anyone.'

She looks so solemn, so vulnerable, that he seeks words to reassure her of his secrecy. 'I promise,' he says, laying the book back down on the table.

'Now,' she says lightly, changing the subject. 'Coffee?'

She pours the hot water into the mugs, stirs them, then adds milk and sugar and pushes his mug across the table towards him. Then she takes two oranges, cuts them into quarters and puts them on a plate. 'They're off the tree out the back,' she offers by way of explanation. 'That's the last of them.'

He watches, sipping at the steaming liquid as she peels several of the quarters. She slips a finger under the peel to separate flesh from pith. From his seat opposite her he can smell the tart tang, can see the minute drops of juice spurt into the air. Finally the segments lie on the plate and she lifts them, one by one, to her mouth.

He finds the slow movement and the way her lips part to taste the fruit strangely erotic. He feels part of him, that hard veneer he's so carefully constructed around himself, flaking slowly away. Unconsciously he wills it back, groping blindly, not knowing why or how. He has the sensation of drowning, or how he imagines drowning to be, a vague indefinable emotion washing over him like warm water.

Meg is talking but, in his bewilderment, he's lost the thread of the conversation. It's something about the wheat and weather, and the way the farmers are slaves to both.

She's thrown her head back and is laughing, a full-bodied solid sound. Her eyes are green and deep-set and crinkled at the corners. Smiling eyes that animate as she talks, understanding and compassionate, as though they might see down to the very soul of him, to that dark place that houses his memories.

His gaze is drawn to the neckline of her dress, its cut low, resting on her collar bone, and he presses back a sudden curious urge to place his mouth there, in the hollow at the base of her throat. Confused, he closes his eyes against the sight of her, pushing away the desire.

He thinks of Susan and the pain rushes back. *I can't do this again*, he thinks, *can't fall in love and let myself be open and vulnerable, especially with another man's wife*. It seems so wrong, a betrayal against one of his own. He needs to back off, walk away. He needs to consign this new awareness to oblivion.

He glances through the doorway. The dark clouds that were gathering on the horizon earlier have come closer and shut out the sun. In the distance he can hear the low rumble of thunder and a sleety rain has begun, shrouding the landscape with a veil of white.

'It's time I was off,' he says abruptly, scraping his chair back against the yellow and black checked lino and picking up her dog-eared exercise book. 'Thanks for the coffee.'

And before she can protest, he is out the door and walking away from her, back to his own life.

Meg sits at the kitchen table and stares at Declan's almost-full mug of coffee. He's hardly touched it, yet already he's gone, down the steps and out into the rain. She can see the hunch of his shoulders and the way he has jammed his hands into his pockets. He's striding purposefully ahead, indifferent to the downpour, and she feels an immeasurable sadness watching him leave. Then suddenly he veers sideways and is lost to view.

Wait, she wants to call. *You haven't finished your coffee.*

But the words die unspoken in her throat and she is left with an ache there and the sense that she might begin to cry.

She could go to the door and watch him as he walks across the paddock, but she presses away the thought. Let him go, something inside her says. Don't torment yourself. He means nothing to you, this man who writes songs and quotes poetry. He's a country singer and soon he'll be gone. Don't let him waken any more of your dreams.

Taking a deep breath, she collects the mugs, rinses them under the tap and places them in the sink. She wipes the table, then she leans back against the bench and closes her eyes. The kitchen seems suddenly quiet with Declan gone. She feels empty and lonely.

In the short time they've spent together, she and Declan have had scant conversation, really, yet she senses that much of what has been left unsaid between them is important. And the fact that she's given him the book of poems, an insight into the very heart of her, tells her more than words ever could. She's laid herself bare before him, and open to criticism. She's made herself vulnerable. What will he think when he reads her words?

She goes to the bedroom and stands in front of the mirror. What does Declan see when he looks at her? She peers forward, frowning at her reflection. Dark hair. Full breasts. Narrow waist and still-trim legs. She supposes she's not bad for her age. Over the years she's looked after herself well, followed a careful diet and exercised regularly.

She unbuttons her blouse slowly and removes her skirt, stripping away the layers of her clothing piece by piece until she stands naked. Tentatively she brings one hand up and runs it lightly across breast and belly, bringing it to rest against the dark triangle of pubic hair.

It's been a long time since she and Grady have made love, months probably, she guesses. Somehow neither of them has the inclination any more, especially not since the last baby – a tiny boy, stillborn, which she gave birth to the year before last. He'd been her miracle child, the only one she'd carried past the first six months. In happy anticipation she'd had the nursery ready with a bright red cot and neat stacks of baby clothes in the cupboard. She'd sat for endless hours in a chair on the verandah, touching her hands to the movements of the child as it rolled inside her and she'd imagined holding him for the first time to her breast.

But nothing went to plan. The doctors weren't able to tell her what had gone wrong and she grieved deeply for months afterwards. Now she suspects Grady stays away from her at night for fear of bringing it all back, the pain and heartache, and because he can't bear another loss himself.

She remembers all this as she sits on the edge of the bed and wraps her arms around herself, rocking back and forward. It feels comforting, the embrace, and she imagines it's Declan's hands holding her and not her own.

Suddenly she's crying hot wet tears that roll unchecked down her face. She's powerless to stop them and doesn't want to, either. Tears for her vanished love with Grady and all those babies she's lost. Tears for her dreams that have never come to fruition. Tears for the monotony and boredom of this place, and a man named Declan who's running from his memories.

She's breathing hard now and fast. Slowly she sags back against the bed, fighting a sense of panic and an overwhelming need for sleep. Where will it lead? Will she ever find peace?

And lying there, her mind teetering between sleep and wakefulness, it seems like ages until her breathing returns to normal.

CHAPTER 11

Magic begins here

At daybreak, Meg Halloran stands at her open living room window and stares out at the rain. It sheets down like a white curtain, flattening the wheat in the paddocks and obliterating the sky. A cold wind blows through it and makes her shiver. Such a change from the past few days, she thinks, as she pulls her cardigan tighter about her shoulders. Somewhere in the guttering, a dawn chorus of frogs honks mournfully.

The rain has reduced Declan's room at the back of the service station to a grey blur. He'll be in there asleep and she tries to picture him lying in the bed. Because of the cold, he'll have the blanket pulled up tight across his back, with only his face and thatch of dark hair showing. The window and door will be closed, with condensation forming on the glass. In her mind she can hear his soft breathing, can see the rise and fall of his chest.

She experiences the desire, sudden and strong, to go and watch him as he sleeps, to look through the uncurtained window and see for herself. All she needs to do is put on her boots and raincoat and she can be there in a few minutes. But what if he wakes and catches her? How can she explain her presence there?

'Stop it!' she cries in the loudest voice she can muster – and then feels suddenly foolish. What is she doing?

She can't stop thinking about him, no matter how hard she tries. At unexpected moments, images of him rise in her mind. Declan pacing up and down beside the truck the first day she saw him. Declan on the night of the barbecue at Connie's, firelight reflected in his eyes. Declan handing her the piece of banded agate yesterday afternoon. *'Chalcedony quartz,'* he said. 'Magicians in Persia used it to divert storms.'

Magicians! It seems Declan is the only one here weaving a spell.

She didn't want to take the stone, but accepting his gift had brought with it the promise of something more, though she wasn't sure what. But he'd stood there, expectantly, holding out his hand. She remembers the shock right through her body when they accidentally touched. And the way she stepped back, for a moment stunned, holding the stone tightly in her own hand.

What's happening? she'd thought then, suddenly not trusting herself or her reactions.

What is going on?

She hasn't slept well – in fact, she's been awake since long before dawn. She'd woken with a start. The room was so dark and quiet, apart from the gentle thrumming of the rain on the roof. There was no snoring from Grady's side of the bed and she'd reached across, feeling for him – but his side was empty. Then she'd remembered.

Now, as she stands watching the rain, she slides one hand into the pocket of her jeans, takes the agate out and holds it. Despite the coolness of the morning, the stone feels warm. As she runs her fingers over its smooth surface, she thinks about a stranger named Declan O'Brien. A travelling man. A country singer. A man who quotes Slessor and Kipling, and makes music from nothing. A man who makes Meg Halloran smile.

A man who is still grieving for his wife and the loss of his future.

So why can't she stop thinking about him?

She's been alone for so long now, in her marriage to Grady and outside it. She's used to her own company, and this need to be with someone, to centre her thoughts solely on him, is overpowering and frightening. She blinks and focuses on the rain. Within a day or so it'll be gone, just like Declan, and the earth will sprout new green shoots and life will go on just the same. It'll be as though he never existed, never trod these tracks and roads, for there'll be nothing left of him to remind her. Except for the memories.

She remembers a poem she once read. She can't recall the title, or the author, but the words, unbidden, come rushing back at her.

Each life is touched,
somehow,
by others,
moulding, forming, singing,
until the solitary singer is
unexpectedly
part of the chorus.

That's what she and Declan are, solitary singers, making their way blindly through life. She with Grady and her lost dreams; Declan with his. What paths have led him to her and, now that their lives have crossed, what effect will the two of them have on each other?

She wills away the thought. The wind catches at the curtains and billows them inwards. It brings with it a spray of moisture. There are chores to be done and take her mind off these fanciful dreamings, so she shivers again and reluctantly closes the window.

Late afternoon, the rain stops. She pulls on a pair of gumboots and, needing to get away from the house even if only for a short time, she steps through the puddles, heading in the direction of the river.

The sun peers through an occasional break in the clouds. Water runs in rivulets downhill to the low-lying areas. Water drips from the leaves of the trees as she passes, splattering around her like bullets as the wind catches them.

Part of her is not surprised to find Declan standing on the bank, watching the rush of water. The river level is up and the surface, all brown and foamy, is littered with the debris of leaf and bark.

'Hello,' he says, watching as she approaches, his hands thrust deep in the pockets of his jeans.

Until now, she hasn't seen him. He's standing in the shade, the dark colour of his clothes merging with the shadow. Yet his voice seems so much a part of the scene that she merely blinks and focuses on him, searching out his details. He's wearing his usual checked shirt – red, this time – and his trade mark jeans. But there's no hat.

'Hello, yourself,' she says. Then she surprises herself. 'Would you like to come for dinner?'

He nods, as she somehow knows he will. 'That'd be nice.'

'Come over at six. I'll make something special.'

She walks away from him, not trusting herself to stay. She wants to keep her thoughts and concentrate on the evening ahead. And why? Why is she doing this? Why is she inviting this stranger into her home? Because, she acknowledges, some part of him, however small, is already in her heart.

She prepares for his visit with meticulous precision, feeling like a schemer. She doesn't know how the events of the evening will unfold, but her instinct tells her that something momentous is about to happen and secretly she hopes she's right. She wants to be prepared for it. She will, she has already decided, accept what happens – and she truly believes that something *will* happen – though she has no idea what.

First she fills the bathtub with warm water and empties her last supply of bath salts into it. The crystals sizzle and spit, settling eventually into a sudsy cloud. Then she lowers herself into it.

She lies with just her head above the bubbles, trying to clear her chaotic thoughts. One part of her wants to run back to the safety and boredom of her life with Grady. It's the life she is familiar with. Too familiar.

But that is her past life, she concedes now.

In just the past two days Declan has woken a restlessness within her, a discontent, and a sense that she needs more. She knows how empty her existence is, how devoid of passion and excitement.

How can she ever again be content with what she has, when she knows now that life has more to offer? She wants to taste it, to experience it. It dances before her, beckoning with an intensity that both frightens and exhilarates her. And whether Declan is the person who can put that lost passion and excitement back in her life, she can't be sure. But she's aware that the loss exists and that she has the emotional capacity for more.

She tries several dresses before settling on a pale green sheath, then she applies just a touch of makeup. Mascara to highlight her long already-dark lashes and a smear of lipstick. A dusting of blusher brings a glow to her cheeks. She gives her hair the standard one hundred strokes, pulling the brush through its thick waves.

She's secretly pleased with the result. The dress is sleeveless and her arms and calves are supple and brown in the dim light of the bedroom. Her hair glows. There's a hint of a smile already playing about her mouth.

Lastly, she dabs her favourite scent – *L'air du temps*, a Christmas present from Connie, who has exotic tastes – behind her ears and knees and slips on a pair of sandals before making her way to the kitchen.

Declan arrives promptly at six, carrying her book of poems and his guitar. He leans the guitar against the wall, next to the door, and lays the exercise book on the edge of the table. Meg waits, holding her breath for a comment, any comment, on the poems.

'They're very good,' he says.

Relief floods through her, followed by doubt. He's teasing, surely, encouraging her.

'You really think so?'

'Yes.'

'You're not just saying that?'

What is she doing: fishing for compliments?

He grins, a smile that crinkles up his mouth and eyes. 'No.'

He leans forward and opens the book at a marked page. For one long moment he watches her, his face solemn. Then he begins to read.

A moment, a fragment,
split second of time.
A dead love, a lost love,
a step out of rhyme.
We woke to the birdsong,
a bright yellow dawn
that shone through our lives
when the dark night had gone...

The words, she knows, are hers, but they sound new. Is that because it's Declan reading them, or because they have taken on a different meaning?

a step out of rhyme...

That's how she feels now. Out of kilter and disoriented. She's wading through an imaginary sea, flailing against an incoming tide that's taking her totally out of her depth. Waiting. Waiting. What will he say next?

She takes a deep breath, willing her heart to stop pounding, wanting to regain her normal calm. But her mind is chaotic. Her eyes rest on the open book, unable to focus. She swallows hard.

He closes the book and the sound, which in reality she knows can barely be heard, is like a drum roll in her head. No one has ever read her poems and she has laid herself open to this man, who is scarcely more than a stranger, by showing him. In one sense, she feels stripped bare and she waits, her hands clammy.

'No, that's really beautiful,' he says, standing back.

She breathes a partial sigh of relief.

'Beautiful,' she echoes, tasting the word. 'You think it's *beautiful?*'

'Poems are like songs. It's all in the way you blend the words, the rhyme you use and the rhythm that the song, or the poem, comes out. I should know,' he laughs, sliding his hands into his pockets. 'I've written and sung some fairly ordinary songs over the years.'

'No!'

She's so certain he could never do anything ordinary, this man who calls her poems beautiful.

'So,' he says, changing the subject. 'What's for dinner?'

He's distracted her and suddenly she remembers the reason for his visit. She's thought hard about what to cook. Fancy or plain? Try to dazzle him with a complicated recipe or stick with the tried and true? In the end, simple seemed easier and she's settled on baby lamb chops and vegetables from her garden.

She pours two sherries from the decanter and settles him at the table. When she finishes hers she excuses herself and takes a basket out to the garden. Her cheeks feel as though they are on fire. Is it the sherry, or the nearness of him? she wonders as she gathers a fresh lettuce and large ripe tomatoes. She cuts a bunch of parsley and shakes the dirt from the lettuce before she takes the basket back inside.

He's sitting at the table, with as much sherry in his glass as when she left. Obviously he's been waiting for her to come back. She lays the basket on the bench and takes the vegetables out. There's a tremor in her hand and she wills it away.

As she takes a pan from the cupboard, he gets up and moves towards her. 'I can help,' he says.

'Really, there's no need.'

'I mean it; I'd like to. I *can* cook, you know. See,' he pats his stomach. 'I haven't starved to death yet.'

Flustered, she pushes the lettuce and tomatoes at him, followed by a sharp knife and a glass bowl. 'Here. You can chop these for a salad, if you like. Just put them all in there.'

It feels odd having someone else – especially a man – working at her kitchen bench. Grady, in the whole of their marriage, has never, ever, offered to help prepare any meal. And if he did, she would suspect his intentions.

'That's woman's work,' he always says, referring to any of her household tasks. Anyway, he never ventures into the kitchen unless it is to take a beer from the fridge or to eat his dinner at the table that is pushed against the far wall.

Macho Grady, she thinks now and feels a small rising tide of resentment towards her husband.

She watches Declan covertly as his hands work deftly with the knife. Chop, chop, chop it goes against the cutting board as he slices the tomatoes into neat even rings and lays them on top of the torn lettuce. He seems comfortable with himself as he moves around with practised ease. Comfortable in her kitchen, she thinks with surprise.

She stands behind him as he works, leaning for a moment on the refrigerator door, letting it take her weight. She can feel the hum of it, the constant vibration. Her gaze moves up to his shoulders, hidden by the freshly pressed shirt, then to the hairs that curl at the back of his neck. They are dark, almost black, and she stifles the sudden and undeniable urge to place her lips there against his warm skin.

Why does she feel this way?

She's never had these thoughts about Grady, never wanted to kiss or touch him except when they're in bed, and seldom then either. She's thought over the years, from the books she's secretly read, that perhaps something is wrong with her, that she has no normal desires, that she is what some might class as frigid.

A shiver runs through her, though she's not certain whether it's from fear or desire. She takes a knife herself and stands beside Declan at the bench.

Inordinately she's aware of his body next to hers, the slow swaying movement as he cuts the vegetables, and feels all fingers and thumbs as she raises her own knife. She also senses his awareness of her and she trims the lamb furiously.

'Slow down,' he says, smiling. 'It's okay. You don't have to rush. We've got all night.'

All night!

The words make her feel light-headed. Her face burns and she dips her head once more to her task.

The thought occurs to her then: how many other kitchens in country towns like this one has this man been in? How many other women has he sliced tomatoes for? How many women have stood behind him, or beside him, thinking the same chaotic thoughts that now churn through her head? The question gnaws, bringing with it a surge of – what? Jealousy? Envy? A spark of resentment?

Then an alternative thought occurs to her. What if this is the first time for him, as it is for her? What if this thing they are now sharing has never been shared before, not with anyone except his wife? She shakes her head.

All she knows is that she feels happy, oddly happy, at having this stranger named Declan, the country singer, in her kitchen. She feels comfortable with him, as one might feel at ease with a worn pair of shoes or warm slippers, as though he has been there for years.

If it had been Grady here, she would have been telling him, 'No, not like that! Do it this way!' But with Declan she feels no need for instruction; simply a calmness about his being in her kitchen, a sense that it is right.

She turns the radio on and there's an old Billie Holliday number playing, something about love gone wrong. She's not listening to the words, but more to the sound of them and the flow of the melody. It makes her feel both sad and happy, this song.

Late afternoon sunlight slants in through the window and slides across the bench, the knife, Declan's fingers. His shirt sleeves are rolled almost up to his elbows. His hands are tanned, dark hairs sprout along his wrists and up his forearms and his fingernails are clipped neatly. She fights the impulse to gather those hands in hers and press them to her face, her mouth.

The urge is so strong, so demanding. What would he think if he knew? He'd probably bolt out the door and take off in his truck, heedless of the repairs needed. Hasn't he told her of the pain of losing his wife, that he can't let himself get close to any woman? Hasn't he said he finds it impossible to let go of the past?

The thought is sudden and insistent. How could she possibly think she can make a difference to this man?

Why? Why her?

At last the preparations are done. The potatoes are simmering in the saucepan and the chops sizzle in the frying pan. She sets the table, laying her best white tablecloth over it and fetching her best plates and cutlery. She's put a small vase of flowers in the centre – pansies and the first of the honeysuckle – and the smell is subtle and pleasing.

'Candles,' he says suddenly, breaking the silence between them.

'C-candles?' she stammers.

'Do you have any?'

Puzzled, she goes to the bottom drawer of the kitchen dresser and pulls out a packet of plain white ones that she keeps for emergencies, like the occasional blackout.

'Will these do?'

'Perfect.'

He takes two small plates from her cupboard and lights the candles, upending them both for a few seconds to allow the first of the melted wax to drip on the plates. Then he settles them upright into the melted wax and holds them steady until it sets.

'Magic begins here,' he says simply.

Meg serves the meal and they sit at the table. 'Lord, thank you for what we are about to receive.' She closes her eyes as she says the words.

They pick up their knives and forks, and begin to eat. The light from the candles flickers and dances on a stray draught of air, and sends shadows spinning up the walls and across Declan's face. Never before has she sat next to a stranger and eaten by candlelight. Yet instead of feeling strange, or wrong, it feels oddly right.

He lifts his fork to his mouth, then stops, grinning wryly at her and nodding at the candles.

'Magic begins here,' he says again.

CHAPTER 12

Free falling

The last time he'd lit candles was at Susan's bedside the day she'd died. Lighting them was symbolic, he'd thought at the time. He and Susan had spent the early days of their relationship talking and playing music by candlelight: all those early sixties songs and artists that now bring back memories, tender yet sad. Buddy Holly. Roy Orbison. Early Elvis. Even then some of the songs, his favourites, still had a fifties feel to them, sort of bluesy and slow, like Henry Mancini's "Moon River". So the lighting of the candles as Susan made her last painful journey was a completion of the circle, a reuniting of the end with the beginning.

He's never even looked at a candle since.

Now, five years later, Declan thinks it's time to bury the demons and end the association. He can't go through life avoiding his emotions forever.

After they have finished eating, Meg clears away the dishes, waving aside his offer of help. Then she fiddles with the radio on the bench, turning the knob. The static crackles back into the room until she finds a clear station.

She seems jittery, distracted, which puzzles him because she's the one who's invited him here tonight. He's reminded of the day he arrived. She'd offered to make his bed and he'd assured her he was quite capable of doing it himself. Did she think it her job, her duty, to attend to all household matters? Did she think it beneath him, unmanly even, to help?

They walk out onto the verandah. The night is dark and moonless and the last of the birds have returned to their nests. A slight breath of wind stirs through the nearby trees. The only light spills through the open doorway from the room beyond, onto the bare verandah boards.

Unbidden, the words crowd into his mind and he says them, slowly, teasing out the sounds. They soar upwards and merge with the darkness, disappearing into the void above.

'*A moment, a fragment,*
split second of time.
A dead love, a lost love,
a step out of rhyme,' he says, looking at the night.

'You remembered the words.' Meg's voice is filled with amazement – or is it delight?

'Like I said, they're good.'

He knows he's repeating himself; he told her earlier in the day. But a part of him needs to reinforce the suggestion.

'There's one thing missing,' she says softly.

'What's that?'

'The words need a tune.'

'You want a tune?'

'Yes.'

She nods and bites her lip.

He considers the request, teetering with indecision. Will he get his guitar? Or should he turn and walk away, keep his feelings intact? The last tune he wrote was for Susan, and for the past five years it's been his dedication to her. Can he change that?

A moment, a fragment…a step out of rhyme.

Suddenly Meg's words seem personal. They're a description of the way he's now feeling: gutted, yet somehow newly alive. He's walking a fine line between the way he's learned to feel and the way he wants to be. He wants freedom, not chains; openness, not this walled-in existence. His emotions are colliding with his commonsense, creating mental chaos.

Part of him wants – no, needs – to back off, return to that shabby room at the back of the service station. Yet it seems the old layers of him are shredding away and unexpectedly he's open and bare. This woman who stands beside him, watching him with her dark eyes and serious face, could take him and twist him, he thinks, mould him into any shape or form and he'd be unable to resist.

He wavers. Then he allows himself to fall, from what has been the black hole of his recent past into the promise of what might become his future. With a nod he takes his guitar from its resting place against the wall next to the kitchen door.

He picks at the strings and the notes slide towards him, towards her, haunting and melancholy. This is not Susan's song, he realises, and it is in no way linked to his past. Instead this is a beginning — this fragment, this step out of rhyme — a chance for a new start and an opportunity to lay his demons to rest.

He picks up the tempo and beats time on the verandah boards with his shoe. Then he smiles at her, this woman named Meg who has somehow made the music come alive inside him again.

Meg can't bear this nearness to him; it's almost like an ache. Panic surges through her. She feels all control sliding away and is powerless to reclaim it.

The last note dies away and Declan leans his guitar against the verandah railing. A sob catches in her throat and her eyes fill suddenly with tears. 'Coffee?' she asks, blinking them away, hoping he doesn't see.

Can he hear the tremor in her voice? *Please say yes*, she pleads silently. If he does, she will have an excuse to go back into the kitchen.

Declan nods, seemingly unaware of her distress. 'That'd be great.'

She walks inside and fills the kettle, flicks the switch. Immediately she can hear it hum. Her hands are shaking and she wraps her arms around herself, willing the sensation to subside. She has to stay calm. Whatever *should* happen *will* happen. This is destiny, or karma, or just plain fate.

But she hates the not knowing, the uncertainty, and a wall of panic rises up inside her again.

She paces, taking cups and placing them on the bench, arranging and rearranging the coffee and sugar canisters. She can't settle, feels distracted, agitated. How can she walk back outside with the coffee? The cups, she knows will rattle on their saucers and declare her nervousness.

She leans against the sink, her breath coming in ragged waves. The pulse at the base of her throat is throbbing. She stares at her reflection in the window. A wild-eyed image mirrors back. Is that really her? How can Declan even look at her face and see sense? Or is there really no difference to her? Is she really only seeing the inside of herself?

She shuts her eyes tight. She can still ask him to go, before she takes total leave of her senses. There is still time to extricate herself from this situation as neatly and as cleanly as possible.

But she knows she has come too far mentally, has already crossed that emotional border. The rest of her days will be bound somehow by this man, if only by the knowing and the memory of him.

The intense need for him has become an ache in her belly. She needs to touch him, *be* touched by him. It need only be the brush of a finger, a slight resting of a hand on her arm, but she needs the physical contact badly.

The jug boils and, taking a deep breath, she pours water onto the coffee granules. Automatically she adds milk and sugar then lifts the cups, not trusting her shaking fingers to place saucers under them, and carries them onto the verandah.

The moon peers around the edges of a cloud. Her shadow sways out across the verandah boards. There's no possible way he can be unaware of her approach, his tanned forearms outstretched and hands gripping the railing as he stares out into the night. Yet he doesn't move, doesn't turn towards her or acknowledge her in any way.

There's the dark curl of his hair again as it rests against his collar and the square set of his shoulders. He seems rigid and she wants to put her hands there, on those shoulders, to massage away the tension she senses has gathered. Again, so caught up is she in his presence that she can scarcely breathe.

She wants to say, 'Talk to me. Tell me what you're thinking.' She wants to know what's on his mind and how it works, the shape and structure of it, but the words are like cottonwool in her mouth.

Instead, she pauses by the door, placing the cups on the low table there. Then she leans against the door frame, unable for a moment to take a step further. To do so, she knows, will take her past some imaginary threshold to a point of no return. There's something there between the two of them, something special and powerful and undeniable. But where will it lead?

On a deep breath she moves forward, placing one foot in front of the other. Her legs feel like jelly, but she wills them on. She places one hand on his shoulder and she can feel the response deep inside him. She rests her hand there, not moving and, at that touch, everything seems to collapse into this one moment.

The awareness of him roars inwards. In the distance, a car starts. Then a dog barks.

Declan turns and smiles.

'Meg,' he says, and the word is like a drawn-out sigh.

She lays her face against his chest and feels the softness of his shirt. Underneath she can feel his heart beating, thumping away in his chest. She feels something shift subtly inside her, realigning itself. Simultaneously she's both standing still and running towards some vague and formless future, balancing on the rim of tomorrow. Giddiness overtakes her and for one awful moment she fears she might fall.

And if she does, where will she land? And will Declan be waiting to catch her?

A shudder runs through her, so intense that she is powerless to control it. Instead she yields to it, turning her face to his, her hands moving automatically to the back of his neck to draw him close.

'Meg,' he says again, the word escaping his mouth, sounding halfway between a whisper and a sigh. For one brief moment it hangs between them, almost tangible, on the air.

He rains kisses, light feathering touches of lips against skin, along her brow and her cheeks. He cups his hand under her chin and tilts her mouth towards his, finds it. She tastes him, long movements of mouth and tongue that leave her aching for more. Then he pulls back and stares into her eyes until she blinks and glances away, trying to focus on something beyond his shoulder. 'Don't,' she says, confused. 'I feel naked when you do that.'

She is falling into him. She feels him press against her legs and belly, the hard prod of him against her thigh. He wants her; she knows that. His body confirms that, as does hers. She raises her face to him again and tastes his mouth.

'Come,' he says, guiding her inside, past the cups of coffee growing cold, back through the kitchen. He takes the two candles and they walk along the hallway. Not to the bedroom she shares with Grady, though. She stops outside the spare room. 'In here,' she whispers, her voice husky.

She's unaware exactly of the process that brings her, naked, to the bed. It has a dreamlike quality, an unreality that she is loath to comprehend. All she is aware of is that she's beside Declan, their skin and mouths touching, fusing.

She begins to feel herself falling again, letting mind and body go. In her mind, she's flying, flying free. Theirs is a slow dance. Mouths meet, exploring the newness, the taste of each other, as his tongue searches for hers. He is, she knows, a man who has been denied for too long.

She moulds her hands to his shoulders, pulling him closer, then she lets them slide down his waist and across his buttocks. 'Oh, God!' he groans, burying his face for a moment against her breast.

She kisses his closed eyelids in the candlelight, wanting to contain past hurt there. Kisses his eyes and nose, forehead and mouth. She moves her lips, lightly brushing, along the side of his neck and he arches against her, searching blindly. She parts her legs and draws him in, and he lets out a long shuddering sigh.

'Oh, God!' he says again. 'Why this? Why now?'

He is moving inside her, ridging his ribs against hers, and she's aware of the weight of him, the smell. Smoke and aftershave, wax, the musky scent of a man. A faint breeze stirs the curtains, sends them fluttering inwards and the candle flame splutters. Shadows dance along the walls and his face. His eyes are dark hollows, familiar yet mysterious.

Slow dance, she thinks. *Slow dance*.

She's reminded of a waltz on a hot summer's night. Not that she's ever experienced that with Grady, but she must have read it somewhere and the idea stirs faintly in her memory.

He bends his head, placing his mouth on her breast, teasing her to hardness with his tongue. There's a flush of heat in her belly and the pleasure rises up, almost pain-like. Pleasure and pain, she wonders, the words are such opposites and she's puzzled that she should link them in her mind.

He takes himself to the brink, then pulls back, attending to her needs as well as his own. She wonders at his endurance (sex with Grady has always been swift and perfunctory) as he whispers in her ear and against her neck, all the while stroking her, pulling her back into him, into *them*.

She feels part of him, joined so tightly as though by some invisible rope, but not just physically; emotionally and spiritually as well. He is her and she him. They are no longer separate but the same, flesh melding and minds entwining.

He's moving faster now, taking her with him. Higher. Higher.

'Come with me, Meg,' he says as though he can read her, like one of her books.

And probably he can.

Just when she thinks she can endure no more, when the pleasure is beginning to consume her, she arches herself under him, dizzying warmth spreading inside. She, who has long since ceased to feel such things, comes again and again.

'Ohhhh,' she cries, her body suddenly rigid. She can't contain her voice within her mouth and her own surprised cry rushes out past teeth and tongue. The sound of it soars up to the ceiling as she sags back against the bedcovers.

It is her signal to him. He poises, rising above her, taking his own weight on his hands, then falls.

He spills himself into her with such intensity that she thinks she might cry out with the wonder, the absolute amazement of it all. He collapses against her shoulder, spent, and she fights the urge to draw him against her breast and cradle him as a mother might hold a child.

Her body is bathed in a film of perspiration. Warmth rushes through her, a dizzying sense of completeness. *Declan*, she says to herself, bringing his face to mind. *Oh, God! Declan. Please don't let me be in love with you.*

'I love you, Meg,' he whispers, as though he can read her mind, and the words are so soft, so indistinct, she thinks for a moment that she might have imagined them.

'Declan,' she whispers, stroking his neck, his chest. She puts one hand behind his head and pulls his mouth against hers. 'Declan.'

The name sounds like music itself, a series of notes that rises to the ceiling. She hears the echoes of it in her mind and tears gather in her eyes, spilling down her cheeks to wet her neck and pillow.

'You're crying,' he murmurs, brushing the wetness away with his thumbs. 'I've hurt you.'

'No,' she blurts out, trying to reassure him. 'Not at all. They're happy tears.'

She's never experienced this completeness, this intimacy before; certainly not with Grady. She's part of this man, has never felt so close to another human, and the feeling engulfs her.

Who is this new Meg Halloran, the woman who has taken this almost-stranger, a man other than her husband, to her bed? She should feel guilt, surely, or some kind of contrition.

But there's nothing except the sense that it is right.

The Country Singer

Later, when her heart stops beating so erratically, Declan lights a cigarette and hands it to her, then lights one for himself. The ends of the cigarettes are red pinpoints in the almost-dark.

There is no need for words as they sprawl among the rumpled sheets in warm companionable silence. *What are words anyway?* she thinks. *They are only noises to fill the space between us.*

He lies next to her, one hand holding the cigarette and the other stroking her breast and belly, light caressing touches that tingle, yet somehow calm. It feels right to be there beside him, she feels part of him, feels the wetness of him between her legs.

She doesn't know what to say. The words won't come and they're jammed, caught between her mind and her tongue. She wants to say she's sorry, though she's not sure why. She wants to tell him that something primal, almost animal-like, shifts her when he touches her.

She wants to say, 'I love you, too,' but this is too soon, too soon. She couldn't possibly be feeling these things. It's the newness, the unpredictability of the situation. In a few days he'll be gone and all she'll have is the memory, the song. She can't let herself love.

The thought of his leaving causes an ache where she imagines her heart to be. Instead, to distract herself, she thinks of the sea and the way he described it to her yesterday.

'On a calm day,' he'd said, 'the water runs up the sand, all gentle-like, then it slides away. On and on it goes, and it's real nice to lie there in the sun, with your eyes closed, listening to the sounds.'

She closes her own eyes now and imagines the waves coursing up the sand, tries to picture it in her mind. And, as she does, the tears come again.

One day she'll go there and she'll witness it for herself. She'll see it all as he's described it. But for now she'll see it through his eyes.

Lying there in the semi-dark, calmed by the cigarette, Declan churns back over the events that have led him to Meg's bed. One minute he was standing by the verandah railing, still unsure of whether to stay or to go; the next she'd walked up behind him.

He'd been aware of her, had seen her shadow sway out towards him and heard her tread on the verandah boards. One step after another, slow and measured, purposeful, yet somehow hesitant and he'd known she was as scared as he was.

She'd placed her hands on his shoulders, pressing lightly. A tremor had run through his body – had she felt it too? – and he'd brought one of his own hands up, covering hers. Then he'd turned and reached out for her, crushing her to his chest. There'd been solace in her nearness and her embrace.

He'd felt the tickle of her hair against his chin, had smelled the scent of her, warm and earthy. She'd met his mouth with her own, opening herself to him. He'd tasted her, long searching movement of tongue and lips that had left him aching for more. Then he'd brought one hand down and cupped her breast, feeling her fullness.

He'd led her to the bedroom, removing her clothing piece by piece, delighting in the unfolding, the revealing, of her body. Then he'd kissed every square inch of it, delighting also in her response. Eventually he'd ridden her, wild and high.

The moment he'd released himself into her, Declan knew the meaning of what had gone before, just as he is now certain about what is yet to come. His future is inextricably joined with hers, and her future with his. She will always hold a part of him inside her.

The moon is fully visible now, a silver orb outside the window. He sees the old ways being taken by a warm September wind to a place where they can be rearranged, where pain fades with time and becomes remembrance and a soft memory.

'We fit together so perfectly,' he says, awed by her body and the way it melds so completely with his.

She nods in the candlelight. Her eyes gleam and he kisses her mouth. And for the first time in his reachable memory, all the pain falls away.

'All these years and all these miles, I've been heading towards you,' he tells her.

New words come, insistent, demanding to be heard. They fill his head and his mouth, spilling into the night air.

'Long forgotten highways,
lonely roads and byways,

searching for you.

You're a face in my dreams.'

'No, I'm not,' she says. 'This is not a dream. It's real. It's happening.'

He feels for her in the soft light and knows what she says is true.

There are just the two of them, no one else in the world, on this September night as the moon glows through the window and the candles flicker to their end.

Outside, the wind picks up and rustles through the nearby stand of bonewood. Some time later, clouds cover the moon again and a few drops of rain fall against the already-damp earth.

In his arms, Meg stirs and sighs, then is still again. Declan knows she is asleep by her breathing and the steady rise and fall of her breast beneath his hand.

'I love you,' he whispers again, surprised once more by the sudden intensity of his feelings.

But this time he knows she cannot hear.

He lies there for a long time, replaying the night in his mind. The dinner. The music. The way her head rested against his chest and the slow waltz of her body beneath his. And when sleep finally comes, he dreams of Susan. But there is no face to her body, there are no features, and he believes in his unconscious heart he has finally put her memory and the pain of losing her, to rest.

CHAPTER 13

A sense of knowing

Meg wakes the next morning – just as she's written in her poem – to the sound of birdsong. There's the warble of magpies and the harsh caw-cawing of a pair of crows. In the distance she can hear a soft kookaburra chuckle.

Declan is asleep next to her. She lies on her side, her head propped on one hand as she watches him. He's so peaceful; his face is relaxed and vulnerable like a child's. Dark lashes rest against his skin His hair is tousled. She wants to reach out and touch it, to run her fingers through it like she did last night. But there's a shyness about her on this new morning, a wariness that confuses her. Instead, she runs one finger lightly along his cheek, barely making contact with his skin. He stirs, but does not wake.

How will they be with each other when he does? she wonders. Part of her is confident, yet another is unsure.

What has she done? She's given herself to this man, both emotionally and physically. Should she feel guilty, now she's broken her marriage vows to Grady? Undoubtedly. Yet, to her shame, there *is* no shame. She's long ago distanced herself from her husband, and where Grady's concerned, she knows there's nothing between them except an unbridgeable void.

Yet, in such a short time, with Declan there's a link, and it's not just the sex, the sharing of that most intimate act. It's a spiritual bond too. Declan understands her, where no one else does. Not Connie. Never Grady. Not even, she considers, her dead parents or those childhood friends who have long since deserted her for the bright city lights. Declan's the only one who understands the *real* Meg, the soft now-exposed core of her.

Tearing her eyes from him, she rolls onto her back and looks up at the ceiling. The early morning sun streams in through the window and its passage through the curtains makes a pattern of lace shadows on the opposite wall. From outside there's the sudden sweet smell of freesias.

For years she's pondered on her relationship with Grady, turning over the pros and cons. Granted, there have been no fireworks, but they've grown comfortable with each other. Comfortable and complacent; content, but in a withdrawn, uneasy manner. Accepting that this life in this town, with the man she chose as her husband fifteen years ago, is her lot – 'once you've made your bed, then you have to lie in it,' hadn't her father had always said? She doesn't have choices. Or does she?

Underneath it all she's always wondered: is this as good as it gets?

She's read about perfect love in her books. That all-or-nothing love, with passions running deep and strong and undeniable. A love that makes you simply want to *be* with someone, to soak in their essence. A love in which a touch means more than a word.

Is that kind of love a fantasy? Can it ever exist, except on the pages of a book or in a fanciful mind?

The question has gnawed at her and never been answered. But now she knows. With Declan it's possible, and real.

Last night she'd experienced emotions she's never felt before. A dizzying wash of desire. The shudder that passes through her when Declan lays his hands on her body. A calmness. A completeness. A sense of *knowing*. She might have been with him for years, so at ease is she in his company, so filled with the soul of him.

She feels new, reborn. As though a hidden part of her is now revealed for all to see. If she leaves this bed and looks in the mirror, will the reflection that stares back at her even resemble the woman she was yesterday, or the day before? Is she still Meg the wife? And what about Meg the lover?

She turns back to him, whispering, 'I don't know who I am anymore.'

He stirs and stretches, then he opens his eyes and smiles at her. 'Good morning,' he says, his voice still thick and lethargic with sleep.

Meg leans across and kisses him on the lips. 'It *is* a good morning, isn't it?'

'We woke to the birdsong and a bright yellow dawn,' he says.

'Mmm.'

She closes her eyes as she listens to his words, *her* words.

'It's like you wrote that for us,' he goes on. 'As though you knew in the past that this was going to be.'

'Maybe I did. Perhaps some part of me knew this was fated to happen.'

'I'm glad it did happen.'

'Me, too.'

He reaches for her and his fingers are on her skin, touching, touching. She grazes her mouth along the side of his neck, his ear. He strokes those places he'd touched last night and she responds, taking him into her, thinking, *this can't be real, this can't be real. Any minute now I'll wake and it'll be Grady lying next to me, and I'll find this has all been a dream.*

But it isn't.

It's fast and sudden. Volatile. Like a thousand tiny shocks exploding through her breasts, her belly. She's flying again, arching against him, stifling a cry, then falling. Declan presses his face hard into her shoulder. 'Meg,' he groans, holding her so tight for a moment that she can scarcely breathe.

For a long time afterwards, she's very quiet, one arm and leg draped across his body. Her thoughts are slipping sideways, teasing her. How often has he done this same thing before?

'Is something wrong?' he asks finally.

It sounds petty and none of her business. His life before this moment is his own concern, isn't it? But she has to know.

'How many women have you woken next to and recited poetry?'

'That's two questions.'

'It is?'

'Are you asking me how many women I've woken up next to, or how many of them I've recited poetry to?'

She considers the question. 'Both.'

'Well, the answer to the first is not many. And the answer to the second is none.'

Relief floods through her and she takes a deep breath. 'There's something else I need to know.'

'Anything. Just ask.'

'Your wife: tell me about your wife.'

'I already have.'

'No. You told me what happened. But what was she like?'

He shakes his head. 'I can't.'

'For everything we shared last night and this morning, I need to know.'

He is silent.

'What was her name?' she asks softly.

He stares hard at her for a moment, then glances away, as though no longer able to meet her gaze. The breeze through the window is warm against their skin.

'Declan?'

'Susan,' he says, his voice harsher than he intended. 'Her name was Susan.'

'Tell me about her.'

'What could you possibly want to know?'

'The colour of her hair, for instance, or the way she smiled. What was her favourite flower?'

He shrugs and rolls onto his back, folding his arms under his head and looking up at the ceiling. Even from that angle Meg can see the resolute set of his mouth. 'It doesn't matter now,' he says.

'Yes it does.' She seizes him by the arm and pulls him back towards her. 'It *does* matter. Of course it does.'

He's silent for what seems like an eternity and when he begins to talk, his voice sounds weary. 'She was like sunshine on a rainy day, if you must know. Her smile was like a rainbow and her favourite flowers were roses. She carried them in her wedding bouquet.'

His voice breaks on that last word, then falls silent. She sees his eyes, bright with unshed tears and wants to wrap her arms around him, to somehow take some of his pain as her own.

'Please, Meg,' he pleads, leaning sideways and brushing a wisp of hair from her face. 'Don't do this. She's gone and nothing can bring her back.'

'But you still have the memories.'

'The memories.' He gives a short mirthless laugh. 'No matter how hard I ran, or how far, I couldn't seem to leave them behind. Then there were some days when I could hardly remember her smile, or how her hair fell about her face. The way I brought her roses and she lowered her face to them, and took in the smell. I took out the photos and scanned them. Memories? Some days I thought I was going mad with the *memories*.'

'The memories are special.'

He pauses for a moment before going on. 'And then I met you.'

He turns to her, blindly, and she takes his hand and raises it to her cheek, holds it there against her skin and knows the warmth, the realness, of him.

It all comes rushing out. He tells her of the places he has been, and the sights – country towns and draughty halls, with applause ranging from half-hearted to thunderous – lonely motel rooms and endless miles travelled in his truck. There's spinifex and gidgee, and a landscape that's dry and barren and stretches to the point where the earth meets a cloudless sky.

As the images tumble into the space between them, Meg can smell the sweet scent of the paddocks, the stale odour of rarely used halls and the musty scent of hotel sheets. She is in the truck with him. The windows are down and warm air is against her face.

It all sounds so wonderful and strangely freeing. She thinks that in a few days time he'll climb into the truck and wave goodbye, and she'll be left here forever dreaming about his life and the thousand country roads he might travel. She'll always wonder whether he's happy and if she's really touched him, as he says. Simply meeting him has changed her own life irrevocably.

His words from the previous day come back to her and they seem so sad, so final.

Long forgotten highways,
lonely roads and byways,
searching for you.
You're a face in my dreams.

He's talking, but she's lost the gist of the conversation, so enmeshed is she in her own thoughts. He's asked something about her parents so she tries to fill the gap, to let him into her life as cleanly as he's allowed her into his.

'When I was quite young, we used to live further west on one of the big cattle runs. There was a drought and all the animals were dying. I remember my father going out each day with his gun and later I'd hear the shots. He was putting the animals out of their misery. We'd sit and watch the sky, my mother and I, wishing the clouds would come and bring rain. But all we got was dust storms, with the sky turning pink and the sand piled up in great drifts on the verandahs.'

She remembers the feeling of abandonment as if it were yesterday. 'Then one day my mother wasn't there. According to my father, she simply walked away. She couldn't take any more of the isolation.'

'What happened to her? Have you kept in touch?'

She shakes her head. 'I never saw her again. We heard years later that she'd died.'

'That's so sad.'

'My father and I came here. He lost everything in the drought and he worked as a fettler on the rail line. We lived in one of the old carriages down at the camp there, and I don't think he ever accepted life in this place. I don't know whether it was the loss of the land or my mother's leaving that destroyed him. He started drinking and –'

Her voice dies away and for a moment she can't go on. He takes her hand, strokes it.

'Anyway, I married Grady and we've tried to make the best of it out here. Most of the kids leave for the city when they finish school and now the place is mostly full of old people.'

'What about friends?'

She shrugs. 'Like I said, most young people leave. I guess Connie's about as good a friend as any.'

'You need to get away sometimes, to have your own independence.'

'Well, in some ways I have. Grady doesn't interfere too much. We have our own space. I've got my books and my poetry. Things could be worse. And I have my dreams. One day I'll travel to the sea.'

'Your independence: don't ever give that up, Meg. And don't lose sight of those dreams either.'

'I won't,' she says drowsily, feeling sleep descend on her again like a dark mantle. It takes her past the void and uncertainty, past all caring. It takes her to the place where she and Declan are one, and also separate, and she welcomes all that with an easy smile.

CHAPTER 14

All the colours of the spectrum

The two of them stand under the hot water of the shower, soaping each other's bodies. Meg runs her sudsy hands over his lean frame, touching those places she did last night and again this morning. He kisses her under the water until they emerge, gasping for air and laughing.

She is cooking breakfast when the phone rings. For a moment she debates whether to answer it, then relents. It's Connie. Her sister-in-law wants to know whether Meg is planning to go to the annual races later in the day. 'Come on, it'll be fun,' she pleads as though she is already anticipating Meg's refusal. 'Everyone will be there.'

'Everyone?'

'Everyone important. Perhaps you could ask your country singer. He *is* still staying at the service station – '

Guardedly, 'Yes.'

She glances across at Declan and frowns. Does Connie suspect?

'Well, are you coming or not?'

Meg makes an excuse. 'No, I think I'll give it a miss this year. I'm not feeling well.'

'Nothing serious, I hope.'

'Just a tummy bug. I was up all night.'

God, she hates lying. Declan looks at her, puzzled, and she smiles at him.

'I'll come over,' says Connie.

'No!' Meg interjects. 'That's not necessary. I'll just take it easy today and I'm sure I'll be fine. Besides, I wouldn't want you to catch it.'

'Well,' says Connie doubtfully. 'If you're sure.'

Firmly, 'I'm sure.'

'Ring if you need me. Promise?'

'I promise.'

She serves up bacon and eggs and thick slabs of toast and cups of milky coffee on the back verandah. She keeps stealing looks at him as he eats, part of her almost not believing what has passed between them or that he is actually in her home, looking like he has lived here forever.

He eats ravenously. Her appetite is gone and she toys with her food. 'Aren't you hungry?' he asks.

She pushes the plate away. 'Not really.'

'Must be that tummy bug,' he jokes.

She offers him a wan smile. 'How old are you, Declan?'

'Thirty.'

'I'm thirty-five. Older than you.'

'Age is just a state of mind.'

'Is it? Do you really believe that?'

He laughs. 'Oscar Wilde once said you should never trust a woman who tells her real age.'

'I have no reason to lie to you.'

'No.'

He rises and walks behind her, wraps his arms around her and buries his face in her hair. 'A man is as old as he feels, while a woman is as old as she looks. Did you know that?'

'So, how old *do* I look?'

'You look like a woman in love, and a woman in love is ageless.'

Making herself weightless against his chest, she leans backwards into him. She feels safe in his embrace and cherished. He hugs her, holding her tight for a moment before releasing her.

'Play for me,' she says, inclining her head towards the guitar there against the verandah wall, abandoned so quickly last night. 'Play me a special song.'

He takes the guitar and draws it to his chest like a lover, just as he held her. She imagines herself against the beating of his heart and savours the soft flood of remembering. She recalls his warmth, the passion rising up between them, taking her to her boundaries and back. She thinks of the way he touched her and how her body arched towards his.

Flying. She was a bird and she was flying.

He picks at one string and the sound breaks the memory. He strums, fingers working against the frets, teasing a tune. She closes her eyes and relaxes against the back of the chair. The words wash over her, lapping her awareness, familiar yet old. Her words. His. Melding together like links in a chain.

He pauses and tightens one of the strings. Then he glances across at her and smiles.

'Don't stop,' she urges.

'*Long forgotten highways,*' he goes on.

'*Lonely roads and byways,*

searching for you.

You're a face in my dreams.'

The last of the notes dies away. 'I'll call it "Meg's Song",' he says softly.

'But it's *our* song: yours *and* mine.'

'Remember the moon?' he asks now, changing the subject as he lays the guitar at his feet. 'Remember how it shone through the window last night and the way the curtains moved in the breeze; how we lay there and let it take place around us and watched it all?'

'What do you think happens when you die?' she asks.

He raises his eyebrows. 'I don't know, but I'm not afraid of death. I'll face it when it comes. Life goes on for everyone left, however painful; I know that. Perhaps it's better to be the one who's died. Susan looked so peaceful at the end. Not scared at all.'

'Her pain was gone.'

A tingle runs down Meg's spine and she shivers. She tries to imagine Declan's hurt after his wife's death, and it mirrors her own when she thinks of his eventual leaving.

'When I die,' he goes on, 'I'm going to be a rainbow.'

'Blue and red, green, yellow and orange: all the colours of the spectrum.'

He looks directly into her eyes, without blinking. 'I've never been able to talk to anyone like I can talk to you,' he confesses. 'It seems so right, so natural. Why is that?'

That evening, they prepare a simple meal.

'Why does this feel so good?' she asks as he sets the plates on the table and lights two new candles.

He takes her in his arms. 'Because,' he says with a smile, 'eating is the most elementary function – without food we die. So if we're going to eat together, we should both contribute to the basics of making that meal.'

'What a wonderful thing to share.'

'Better than this?'

He bends his head and teases his mouth the length of her neck. Suddenly the meal is forgotten as she pulls his lips towards her own.

'Kiss me,' she commands. 'Kiss me properly.'

CHAPTER 15

Distant horizons

'How do you know when someone's right for you?' asks Declan the next morning as they lie in a warm tangle of arms and legs. Already the day promises to be a hot one and the breeze coming in the window covers Meg's face with a sheen of perspiration.

He thinks for a while. 'When it feels right. And this feels so right, Meg – you and I.'

'But what if there's someone out there who's perfect, more suited?'

'There are probably a thousand perfect people out there, for each of us. But will we ever meet them?'

'Perhaps not.'

'And what if they all live in China or Russia?'

'Well, I guess we'll *never* meet them, then.' She laughs at the absurdity of the thought, knowing the truth of his words.

'You're right.'

'So it's chance, fate, karma. A what-will-be-*will-be* kind of thinking,' she agrees. 'That perfect person could pass you on the street and you'd never know because you wouldn't even have the chance to speak to them.'

'It's the meeting that makes the difference. The right person is the one who, metaphorically speaking, you happen to sit next to on the bus. You strike up a conversation because the opportunity's there. Something about the weather perhaps, or the fact that the driver is late.'

'Or the reason you even have to catch the bus in the first place.'

'Exactly.'

'I'm glad you got my bus then,' she says, suddenly shy.

'Hey,' he says, tilting her face towards his and kissing her soundly on the lips. 'You're driving this bus, pretty lady. I'm a passenger – and a not unwilling one at that.'

Connie calls in unannounced, mid-morning. Meg has just put the kettle on the stove and is spooning instant coffee into two mugs.

'I can see I'm just in time for a cuppa,' says the older woman, breezing into the kitchen without knocking. She lets the screen door slam in her wake. Then, as her eyes adjust to the dimmer indoor light, she notices Declan sitting at the table, his long legs stretched in front of him.

'Oh, hello,' she says hesitantly, then to Meg, 'I see you have company.'

Over coffee, Connie entertains them with the events at the races yesterday. She describes the people and the absurd hats some of the women wore. 'You'd think it was the city! Such silliness. I wore my old Dolly Varden. You know, the pink one with the cabbage roses.'

'Connie! That's ancient!'

'Yes, I know. Not the height of fashion, but it's comfortable. Anyway, you should have seen the looks I got. But you missed a great time,' she tells them. 'Unfortunately it wasn't my lucky day. The horse I backed is still running.'

Declan laughs, more out of politeness, Meg thinks, than amusement, as Connie prattles on. There's something about her sister-in-law today that's brittle and wary, as though she suspects something but can't quite put a name to it. She keeps glancing at Declan in a mistrustful way. Clearly, she wants to know what he's doing here.

'Actually, Meg, I came up to ask you to dinner tonight. I thought you might be lonely, what with Grady being away. But I can see I was mistaken.'

Deliberately, Meg doesn't look at Declan. 'That's a lovely idea, Connie, but I thought I'd have an early night – '

'Oh, I forgot,' says Connie, a hint of sarcasm in her tone of voice. 'The tummy bug yesterday. That's right.'

'It's not that. I've – '

Connie cuts Meg off for the second time. 'So, what's wrong with your truck?' she asks Declan. 'Why can't you get it to the next town? It'd be better to do that than wait for Grady to get back.'

'Better?' He frowns.

'Better,' she says firmly.

He shakes his head. 'I'm not sure. Mechanics isn't exactly my strong point.'

'Well, then.' Connie gets up out of her chair. 'Let's have a look at it, shall we?'

'Sure.' He shoots Meg a puzzled glance as he follows Connie to the door. Meg shakes her head.

She watches the two of them walk across the paddock to where the truck is parked in the shade, next to the room behind the service station. Declan puts the bonnet up and Connie bends in under it.

Panic rushes up inside Meg's chest. What if Connie says something to Grady about Declan being in the house? Not that she would on purpose – Connie is not usually nasty or manipulative – but it might slip out accidentally in conversation. How would she explain to Grady, without getting flustered and arousing suspicion?

The full implication of what she's done niggles at her. She busies herself collecting the empty mugs and rinsing them under hot water. She can't stop thinking about Declan's eventual leaving and how she will say goodbye. How can she stand the thought of him walking away and of never seeing him again? *Breathe,* she tells herself. *Breathe deep and slow.*

When she looks at the truck again, she can see old Horace there, from the general store. There's much pointing and leaning against it, arms folded and constant nodding.

What's happening? She is suddenly suspicious of Connie all over again.

She is still busy at the sink when Declan comes in and wraps his arms around her. 'Come with me, Meg,' he says against her ear.

She thinks she's heard wrong. *Come with me:* what is that supposed to mean? Go with him *where?* 'Where?' She is confused.

'Come with me and be with me, when I leave here,' he says, turning her towards him. He stares into her eyes as though daring her to say no. 'The old bloke from the general store reckons I'll get through to the next town, no worries. Says the noise coming from the truck is something to do with the motor, but it's not in imminent danger of breaking down.'

He holds her at arm's length. For one agonising moment she can't look at him, can't meet his gaze. He places one finger under her chin and lifts her head. 'I never expected to feel this way again,' he goes on. 'About you. About any woman. I can't walk away from you.'

'Declan,' she says faintly, shocked, not believing what he says.

'As Robert Browning said: "Grow old along with me! The best is yet to be".'

'Do you really believe that?'

'What I do believe is that all the roads I travelled these past five years, all the directions I've headed and the byways I've taken, were all detours leading me to you. It just took a while to find you, to find *us*, that's all. And now that we've found each other, we should travel the rest of those miles together.'

She looks at him sadly and shakes her head. 'I can't.'

'Meg,' he says urgently. 'Come with me and I'll take you to those places you've never seen. I'll write songs for you. I'll sing for you.'

He buries his face in her neck and for one long moment is still. She holds him and can feel the thump-thump of his heart. He is breathing hard, like a man who has run a long race.

'Declan,' she says again faintly.

'I'll take you to the sea and I'll show you where the water runs up the sand,' he says at last, pulling away, 'where the blueness of the ocean is so intense it makes your eyes ache.'

She shakes her head hesitantly, thinking of Grady and Connie. How could they ever understand? Besides, this town is the only place she has known in her adult life.

Yet the need inside her is pure and strong and she senses a freedom she has never thought possible. How would it feel to ride high in Declan's truck, with the wind wild in her hair? What would it be like to pull up in strange towns and lie in strange beds – to make love with Declan between those strange sheets – with the man she now knows she loves?

In her mind's eye she sees distant horizons and a seashore.

'Come with me,' he says again. Somehow she senses it will be the last time he asks and she must make a decision. Yes or no.

Her own life has been inexorably altered over the past few days, and her marriage to Grady has been rendered trivial and inconsequential. All of her being is now in Declan, and his in her. She senses that, *knows* it. Something binds them, some cords or chain, or thoughts and beliefs. She is powerless to analyse it into something tangible and meaningful, because it's not that simple. It is sacred and spiritual. There are no words to define the way she feels because she has never felt these things before and they are foreign and confusing.

She is poised on the edge of something monumental, she knows that. Poised and ready and willing to fall. And the need to experience that sensation is strong in her.

Grady could survive without her. Apart from having no one to wash and clean and cook for him, he would go on in much the same old way. But if she stays, she might die of suffocation here; her heart and spirit and reason for living might simply shrivel and disappear.

'Where will we go?'

He glances at her sharply, his features revealing his surprise at her question.

'Where do you want to go?'

'I don't know. Anywhere. Everywhere.'

'Life's a journey, Meg, that's all I can tell you; not a destination. I don't know where we'll end up. But if you say yes we'll make that journey together.' He reaches for her hand and lifts it to his mouth. 'With all of my being, I beg you. Come with me and we'll make a life together.'

The future expands before her, encompassing all her thoughts, and him. Knowing her own future is somehow entwined with his, needing him and knowing part of him needs her too, she can't be without him.

'Yes.'

She sees him sag with relief. 'You won't regret it, Meg, I promise you that.'

Later that afternoon she lays her clothes on the bed she shares with Grady and considers them. There aren't many; just the basic necessities. But she has some money saved and plans to buy some new ones when they reach a place with decent shops.

Now that she has made her choice, Declan decides to risk the truck. They'll drive to the next town and effect the repairs there, so they'll be gone a couple of days before Grady's expected return. 'The truck has made it this far,' he tells her. 'Hopefully it'll take us those few extra miles.'

So she's only taking a few clothes, some photographs and books. Not much for a lifetime. But she'll be starting on a new life and wants to leave as much as possible of the old behind.

She stands in the middle of the room, twisting the wedding ring on her finger. It seems silly to take it with her: after all, she's renouncing that married part of her life.

Suddenly she pulls it over her knuckle and drops it onto the top of the dressing table. The ring spins on its edge for a few seconds, slowing as it does, until it falls onto its side with a *kerthunk* and lies still.

Declan has gone to his room to shower and pack. Meg hears footsteps on the verandah. *Declan,* she thinks, surprised at his speedy return. But it's Connie standing there in the bedroom doorway, with her hands on her hips.

'What are you doing?' she snaps, eyeing the clothes and suitcase.

How can Meg explain her decision so that Connie will understand? 'I can't stay here,' she says and the words seem hopelessly inadequate.

'Why not?'

'My life with Grady, this town: it's all mindless monotony. There has to be more than this.'

'And you're going to find it with Declan?'

Meg nods.

Connie walks across to the dressing table and picks up Meg's wedding ring, weighs it thoughtfully in her hand. 'So, you're leaving,' she says. 'What about Grady? It'll destroy him if you go.'

'It'll destroy me if I stay.'

'It can't be that terrible, surely.'

'I feel like I've lost myself, somewhere between Grady and this place.'

'It's not all bad, being here,' Connie says defensively.

'No.' Meg needs to explain. 'But I have to see other places, to live another life. I feel like I'm drowning, or running backwards, or something.' Suddenly she buries her face in her hands as the tears come, fast and hot. 'Don't hate me, Connie.'

'I don't hate you. In some ways I wish it was me leaving.'

'With Declan?'

Connie smiles. A sadness crosses her face for a moment and is gone. 'So you've made your mind up? This is really what you want to do?'

'Yes.'

After Connie leaves, Meg stands on the front step and looks out over the countryside. The wheat fields shimmer in the golden light of the late afternoon. A flock of birds flies overhead, shrieking loudly. She hears the slam of a door and looks across to the service station where Declan is loading his guitar and suitcase into the back of the truck.

She thinks of Grady and wonders what his reaction will be when he finds her gone. It'll be up to Connie to help him cope. It'll be a different kind of life, being on the road with Declan. But she's made the decision and there can be no looking back, no regrets.

'The music will be gone from this place when you leave,' Declan says, coming over to her now and wrapping his arms around her. She sways against him, feeling the strength of his body and the way he supports her. This man, she knows for certain, will never let her fall.

It comes to her then, as she looks across the paddocks, that she is not alone. Instead she's an infinitesimal part of some whole, a mere speck in the scheme of creation. She imagines life spiralling into the future, limitless, on and on, long after she and Declan have crumbled into dust.

We are born and we will die, she thinks and strangely the idea reassures her. She knows suddenly that if life is like a song, then she is simply part of the chorus, a repetition of all that has gone before and all that will follow. Like drought and flood: each is a chorus, too, repeating itself in no particular pattern or rhyme.

The sun has disappeared behind a bank of clouds and thunder rumbles softly in the distance. She takes a deep breath, inhaling the faint sweet smell of approaching rain, and smiles.

Rain: the most important chorus of them all, replenishing the dry earth, drawing tiny green shoots upwards for tomorrow's sun.

The only difference is she won't be here to see it.

Declan stands before Meg, holding her tightly as she gazes across the land for what he knows is the last time. He buries his face in her hair and inhales the fresh smell. It's time they left. The rain clouds are banking up above the fields of wheat. There are drum-rolls of thunder overhead.

He takes it all in, almost not believing the past few days. All the country roads he's travelled, all the miles he's left behind and all the distance yet to go haven't prepared him for this: the unexpected intensity of feeling; his need for her. Why Meg? And why now?

He allows the thought to float as he tries to find the shape of it.

In a few minutes they'll climb in his truck and, God willing, they'll make it to the next town down the line. He knows he can't leave her here, can't leave without her. In this place she's drowning and he has to save her.

He can't imagine what the future might hold. All he knows is that he wants her with him; he wants to sit in his truck with her and write songs for her, and he knows that the old Declan has finally crawled out of that self-imposed exile and is ready to face life again.

CHAPTER 16

Deception and lies

Meg writes a note to her husband to explain why she is leaving – she owes him that much for the fifteen years of marriage they have shared. The reasons don't come easily. How will she make him see that she has to leave for her own sanity and sense of self? How can she put in plain words the reason she feels their life together has become like a death?

She seals the note in an envelope and writes 'Grady' on the front in capital letters, then props it up on the top of the dressing table next to her wedding ring. He can't fail, she thinks, to see the significance of that. Then she closes the suitcase with a snap and clicks the locks shut.

For the last time, she walks through the house, her gaze lingering on ordinary little things. Two cigarette stubs in the ashtray on the verandah. The spare bedroom where she and Declan made love – the cover pulled straight on the bed, leaving no sign that anyone has been there. The stubs of two candles sitting on the dining room table. A scuff-mark in the dust on the verandah boards where Declan's guitar rested. She takes them all in and stores them neatly in the back of her mind. This is how she will remember the place.

She hears Declan start his truck. It turns over several times with an odd protesting sound. She thinks, *If it doesn't start, then it's an omen, a sign that I'm supposed to stay*.

But it catches on the fourth turn and she breathes out in a long sigh. *This is meant to be, then.*

Closing the front door behind her, she walks down the front steps. Declan hoists her suitcase onto the back of the truck, next to his own and the guitar, and throws a tarpaulin over the lot. 'Ready?' he asks with a smile and holds the door open for her.

She settles herself nervously in the seat, watching as he puts the truck into gear and releases his foot from the clutch. The vehicle slowly grinds forward, pulling from shadow into sunlight. His capable hands on the steering wheel guide the truck through the paddock that separates the service station and Meg's home – or *former* home.

They pass the service station and she closes her eyes for a moment against the sign – *Halloran's Service Centre Est. 1955*. The bowser is dusty and already the place has a neglected air. They pass other houses, other lives going on. The late afternoon sunlight glints on the river ahead and suddenly they're passing Connie's place. Her sister-in-law sits on the verandah, watching. She doesn't nod or wave, simply stares at the truck until Meg blinks and looks away.

I'm sorry, Connie, she says silently to herself. *I'm sorry.*

They're on the outskirts of town now. The silos and the grain elevator flash by. All that stretch in front of Declan's truck are the seemingly endless paddocks of wheat and the road that leads to her future.

He lifts one hand from the wheel and takes hers. 'Happy?' he asks.

'Yes.'

She is staring at him and, for a moment, she doesn't see the dog run out onto the centre of the road. She only hears Declan curse as he drops her hand and grabs the steering wheel again. She sees the back of the mongrel as it disappears under the front of the truck. There's a thud – an awful dull sound – and the truck rears upwards. She hears her own intake of breath.

Everything seems to happen in slow motion. The truck skids sideways. She can feel the swerve of it, can hear the crunch of tyres across the gravel. It's bucking under them like a rodeo bull. Then they head over the shoulder of the road and into a deep ditch.

A tree looms ahead. It's straight and tall, broad. Meg can see the bark, the furrows and indentations. From the corner of her eye, she sees Declan wrenching at the wheel. He pulls it savagely towards him, trying to spin the truck away. She braces herself for the impact.

She's powerless to stop the scream as it escapes her mouth. It's driven by fear and shock. 'Declan! Oh my God, Declan!'

At the last moment the truck slides in a right turn. Meg's door is no longer heading for the tree. There's an explosion of steel. It's louder than anything she's ever heard before, followed by a grinding shriek that seems to go on and on.

Then everything comes to a dead halt.

Meg's body flies forward. Her head collides with something hard and unyielding. Pain stabs. For a moment everything goes black. Why is that? It's still late afternoon and the sun is shining, isn't it?

Vaguely, she's aware of her own screams. Over all there's a stench of petrol and dust and rubber, and a metallic burnt odour. Everything spins around her. Smells and noises clash violently in her head, bleeding together like some horrible nightmare.

Suddenly she's floating, soaring up towards the sun. From her vantage point she looks down on the truck. Somehow it has managed to turn one-hundred-and-eighty degrees and the metal of the driver's door is wrapped around the tree.

Something is very wrong. Declan is sitting in the driver's seat, upright and absolutely still. A trickle of blood runs down his forehead. From that height, Meg sees herself reach over and shake his arm.

'Declan, speak to me!' she hears herself scream.

There's an urgency in her voice, a need for him to respond. But he just sits there and the blood runs down, and out of his mouth and ears.

Then everything goes black again.

Connie sits on her verandah and stares after the truck. A cloud of dust kicks up behind the rear wheels. Through the rear window she can see the two of them, Meg and Declan, sitting upright and tall. *Grady!* she thinks, feeling nauseous. *How will I tell him?*

She's about to get up and go inside when she hears the distant thud. From a far-off stand of trees, a flock of birds lifts into the sky in one shrieking mass. A dog howls and then all is quiet.

Something is wrong. She can feel it. 'Please God,' she says quietly to herself as she runs and runs to the sound.

She can't believe the tangle of metal and rubber. The truck, or what's left of it, is wrapped right around the tree. For Declan, she's certain it's too late and, through the shattered glass of the driver's window, she places her finger on the base of his throat, searching for a pulse. There is none.

Meg is alive, although covered in blood. Her forehead is swollen beyond all recognition. Carefully Connie eases her out of the wreckage and sits her on the grass, well away. There's an overpowering smell of petrol and she's afraid there might be a fire.

Meg's shaking, badly. She's in shock, her mouth moving, though no words come out. Connie knows there's no way her sister-in-law can walk, and she needs medical attention. There are cuts on her face that probably need stitching. So she sprints back to her own cottage for her car.

She's about to drive away, heading for the hospital, when she sees Meg's suitcase. It's lying on the ground, obviously thrown from Declan's truck by the force of the impact. The lock has broken and the lid is undone. Clothing and books sprawl untidily across the road. Thrusting the gear lever into neutral, Connie gets out and scoops up the belongings and case, then dumps them in her own boot.

No one needs to know what was happening here.

After she makes certain Meg is being well taken care of by the doctor, and that her injuries aren't life-threatening, Connie takes the suitcase back to Grady's house. She unpacks the clothes and books. She empties the ashtray on the verandah, and hides the remains of the candles at the back of the cupboard under the sink. Then she goes back to the hospital and sits by Meg's bed until she wakes.

Grady arrives back in town two days later.

'What happened?' he asks Connie after he has been to see Meg. 'No one at the hospital seems to know.'

Connie tells him an abbreviated version of the events of the past week. 'I know he needed to get to the next town. He was a singer and he had a gig there. Perhaps Meg was driving him to the railway siding?'

Grady glances sharply at her. 'Why would she do that?'

Connie shrugs, and feels suddenly like crying. She hates deception and lies but there seems no other way. 'I'm sure she was just helping him out, that's all. She was probably going to bring the truck back here for you to fix.'

He frowns. 'But the accident happened out the other side of town, not near the siding at all.'

Connie gives him a long hard look and shakes her head, for the moment unable to speak.

'Was she leaving with him?' Grady asks, his voice breaking.

'For God's sake,' she says, turning her face away. 'Just don't ask! She's alive, and that's all that matters.'

CHAPTER 17

Hiding the truth

2005
The wheat fields, Western Australia

'Oh, my God!' I say, and the words bounce back at me, stark and real, from the hospital room walls.

'Gemma,' says Aunt Connie. 'Are you all right?'

I shake my head. 'Yes. No,' I say, unable to make up my mind. Then, 'I don't know.'

'It's all been a bit of a shock for you,' she adds.

I feel a pressure at my temples and start rubbing absent-mindedly. The walls, Aunt Connie and her bed, blur together in a mish-mash of colour. In my mind's eye I visualise the wreckage of the car lying beside the road. I can see Declan's body sitting upright behind the steering wheel and my mother crying, calling for the return of her dreams and her future with the man who had so neatly stepped into her life, then out of it.

'There was a police investigation,' Connie adds, 'but nothing ever really came of it. In a one-horse town like this, where everyone knows the other's business, you'd think it'd all eventually come out. But I managed to hide the truth. Clever, wasn't I?'

Aunt Connie lies in her hospital bed, tears streaming down her own face. Her voice has broken to a whisper, getting softer and softer as the story progresses until there's no sound at all coming out her mouth. I put my hand on hers. 'Don't,' I beg, more concerned for her maybe than myself. 'Don't go on.'

The telling of the story is breaking her into tiny pieces.

'I have to, Gemma. You need to know the truth.'

'The truth? That my mother was in love with another man? That she was planning to leave my father?'

The tone of my voice is harsher than I'd intended and she winces.

'The truth,' she repeats in a shaky voice. 'You haven't heard it all.'

CHAPTER 18

Afterwards

Every morning Meg wakes to a nightmare that won't go away. There are days when she's in a black hole, trying to claw her way up and out. Sometimes she thinks she can't survive another hour. Declan has shown her another kind of life, one she's never shared with Grady, and the accident has not only removed him physically from her, it has snatched away her future as well. Now her own life stretches before her, bleak and hopeless. Inexorably all her expectations have been altered.

When she arrives home from hospital she finds that the few things she was taking away with her have been unpacked, and the suitcase with its broken lock and scoured surface has been put back on the top of the wardrobe. Connie has done it. Meg knows, because her sister-in-law has told her so.

There's a dark emptiness inside her, an accumulation of grief and guilt that, as time passes, blur into each other. There are days when she aches for Declan's touch. The wanting becomes a physical pain.

Then there are days when her memories are so incomplete, so fractured and torn, that she wonders if she has made it all up. Perhaps Declan only exists in her imagination and the accident is nothing more than a bad dream. But she just has to look in the mirror, at the scars and scratches and bruises fading from purple to dark yellow, to know that it's all real. And if that is not reassurance enough, she can force herself to walk to the yard at the rear of Grady's service station and see the tangled twist of metal that was once Declan's truck. Then the reminders come screaming back

Only once does she venture close to the wreckage. She bends down to look inside. The roof has caved in over the space where Declan's head had been. The dashboard is pushed back into the cabin and the windscreen is a jagged, shattered mess. Shards of glass cover the seats and the floor. The concave shape of the tree is forever imprinted into the driver's door. Nausea builds inside her belly as she notices the rust-coloured stains on the seat inside that door: Declan's blood.

One afternoon she walks out on the verandah. A thunderstorm is approaching and the sky on the western horizon is black and bruised with clouds. Thunder grumbles and she's reminded suddenly of Declan and that other storm, and the poem he quoted.

She says Slessor's words softly and lets them fall about her. The memory causes the pain to well up unbearably inside her and she looks up, blinking back sudden tears, towards the sky.

There's a rainbow above her.

No! Her heart is pounding. There are two! Twin coloured arcs, one above the other, beginning and ending at almost the same point.

'When I die,' Declan had said, 'I'm going to be a rainbow.'

She can remember his embrace, can almost feel his arms around her. She's lived her whole lifetime in those few short days they'd shared, her entire existence encompassed by the presence, and now the absence, of him.

All the colours of the spectrum, she thinks, sorting the rainbow tones before her, trying to separate them. But they flow together in sudden tears. All at once she's sitting on the ground, with her head in her hands, sobbing as though her heart will break.

One day, while Grady is at work, Connie arrives unannounced on Meg's doorstep. Her sister-in-law has been conspicuous lately by her absence, and the once-easy familiarity between the two women has been strained.

'Why did you really leave?' she asks Meg as they sit at the kitchen table, sipping coffee. 'I need you to explain it to me so I can understand.'

'I'm not sure I can,' replies Meg guardedly. She's loath to discuss that day, scared of the pain the memories will bring.

'Weren't we enough for you?'

'Because I loved him,' Meg says simply. 'And I didn't love Grady.'

'What could he have done that Grady didn't?'

'Besides love me?'

'In his own way, Grady has always loved you. He still does.'

Meg knows the truth in that. 'Declan was going to take me to the sea.'

'The sea?'

Connie shakes her head and Meg changes the subject. They talk about the weather and the successful wheat harvest, and the news that the road east might be widened and tarred soon.

'It's better to have loved and lost, than never to have loved at all,' Connie tells her pragmatically as she leaves.

'Well,' Meg answers, her heart torn apart. 'Whoever said that hasn't recently lost.'

'I'll never speak of this again,' Connie says. 'To you or Grady.'

Meg spends the following weeks healing her body and her heart, for both have been broken. She finds the remains of the candles in the cupboard under the sink where Connie has hidden them. Immediately she's reminded of the night Declan lit them and the way the flames rose up straight and tall.

'Magic begins here,' he said. But now, looking at the stubs and the way the cold wax had run and puddled into a congealed mass, she is reminded only of tears.

Then, one day, the truck wreck is gone and it is as though it has never existed. Nothing is left in the space it once occupied, except for a few straggly weeds that have grown up around the deflated tyres, and a large oil stain.

Yet, despite her grief, as the weeks slowly pass Meg is aware of a change, a shifting inside her. Somehow, despite the trauma and the wounding of body and spirit, another baby grows there, inside her darkness. She waits, pressing her hand against her belly at odd times.

This is a miracle, she thinks, part of her excited yet another quite panicky at the possibility of losing it, as she has lost all the others.

'We are all responsible for our own happiness,' Connie says the day Meg tells her the news about the child. 'This baby is a gift. Treasure it.'

It's true, Meg concedes to herself later. She can't let Declan's death ruin her whole life. She has given herself permission and time to grieve, and when that time passes and she has mended emotionally and spiritually, she'll stop and move on. And this child – Declan's baby – will help her.

It is a cold blustery day the following June, when Declan's baby is born with almost no fuss at all. Meg feels the first contractions around midnight and Grady takes her to the hospital. She paces the corridors, breathing hard and fast, praying that nothing goes wrong. By dawn the last is over. One hard push and the tiny body slides onto the sheets between her legs. Miraculously the pain melts away and fades to a memory.

'It's a girl,' the doctor says, holding her up and slapping her bottom. The baby cries, a thin wailing sound, and they place her in Meg's arms. She experiences a surge of love so strong, so pure, that she thinks she might cry out with the joy of it. 'Gemma,' she says. 'We'll call her Gemma.'

She sees Grady hold the little girl for the first time and feels immeasurable sadness. He knows the child isn't his, yet he's said nothing, apportioned her no blame. Over the downy head of the child, in that austere hospital delivery room, he raises his eyes to hers. *I'm sorry,* his expression says. *Meg, I'm sorry.*

CHAPTER 19

September moon

It takes more than a year, but at last Meg feels she's emerging from a long dark tunnel into light. In many ways, the monotony of her life in this town with Grady makes her want to scream. Declan led her, if just for a few days, into another life. He allowed her a taste of the way things might have been. She glimpsed alternatives and options, a mere sliver of another life. But in the end, after Declan's death, she knows she has rejected them also.

She suffers from occasional headaches, and back pain becomes a daily grind. It's from the accident, she knows, but the suffering seems small compared with his. Gemma is a delight and she is comforted by her, her grief subsiding as the weeks and months pass, made more bearable by the distraction. She watches Grady play with a child that isn't his, though he never says a word. Not one. No accusations. No questions. And it is, as time passes, as though those few days with Declan never happened.

She supposes, in her nostalgic moments, that she could take Gemma and leave this place. But where would she go? This town and these people are all she knows. So she stays, self-contained and absorbed in her daughter, pressing the thoughts of that non-existent future with Declan into the far recesses of her heart.

She buys a fresh packet of candles. One day, while Grady is at work and Gemma is sleeping, she places two on the kitchen table and lights them, waiting for the wall of pain to come rushing back. It is still there, she knows, and will probably never go away. But it is dulled now, made softer around the edges by the passage of time.

They are, she tells herself, only candles after all.

On the anniversary of her meeting with Declan, she takes the poem they wrote together – "Meg's Song" – and goes to the room at the back of Grady's service station. She lights another two candles, lies on the blue-and-white-striped ticking of the mattress and reads the words.

She stays there for a long time, remembering, unexpected snatches of memory hurtling back at her. Declan standing on the verandah that first night they made love. Declan strumming his guitar. The way he touched her, stroking her mind and body into new emotions.

Then she folds the piece of paper and stows it in her pocket, blows out the candles and leaves, closing the door behind her.

It is her ritual, her way of grieving and resolution.

Meanwhile, she watches her daughter grow. Gemma at six weeks with her first smile. Gemma at six months crawling across the yellow and black lino. Gemma at six, looking like a smaller and finer version of Declan ‹ dark hair and indigo eyes, and the way she has of flicking her hair back as she talks. God! Some days it hurts so badly just to look at her!

The arguments with Grady are constant. At the end of one, she twists her wedding ring off her finger (Connie suggested, delicately, that she start wearing it again after the accident) and throws it after him as he goes out the door. It hits his back, but he doesn't even pause in his stride. Has he even felt it? The gold band bounces on the floor, spins slowly for a moment, then falls on its side.

Suddenly she's reminded of that other time, the day she left with Declan, when she'd placed the ring on the dressing table

The ring lies there for two days on the carpet, neither she nor Grady bothering to pick it up. Finally she gives in, puts it back on her finger and knows as she does that she accepts the finality of her situation. She will stay there, in that town, and be Grady's wife. There is no other choice.

The headaches become worse when Gemma is eight and some days Meg has to take to her bed. Grady nags her to see the doctor though at first she resists. As the weeks pass, however, she feels herself slipping. The pain in her head becomes increasingly unbearable and the easiest tasks more difficult.

Grady takes her to the next town. There are tests, banks of them, then the prognosis – something malevolent is growing inside her head, pressing against sensitive parts.

'Inoperable,' says the doctor. 'Too much risk and too little chance of success. In my opinion, it's possibly a result of the accident.'

She tries, how she tries, to carry on as normal. But as the days slide past, her world seems tilted, out of kilter. Her thoughts run in circles, the ends of them joining up with the beginnings. Her co-ordination skews. Eventually she finds it difficult to walk, even to place one foot in front of the other. Connie comes every day to help with Gemma, to get the little girl ready for school, and stays to do odd jobs around the house.

'I'm being punished,' Meg tells her sister-in-law.

'Punished for what?'

The words won't come and anyway Meg's not sure she can fully explain, even now, that special bond she and Declan shared, and the way she was willing to leave everything behind, just to be with him. 'You know,' she says instead, unable for a moment to meet Connie's gaze.

'I don't blame you any more,' says Connie quietly, 'if that's what you think. Oh, I know I did at first. I was hard and cold. But time lessens all feelings.'

'Just don't pity me now, okay?'

Connie glances away, but not before Meg can see her eyes bright with unshed tears.

Two days later, the wheelchair arrives on the mail plane. 'Come on,' says Connie practically, helping her into it. 'I'll take you for a spin.'

The Country Singer

Desperately, Grady takes Connie aside. 'She's like a caged bird,' he says to his sister, 'but I don't know how to set her free.'

'You *can't* set her free, you mean.'

He shakes his head. He looks like a drowning man.

'There's nothing more to be done, you know that,' Connie says. 'All we can do is wait and hope the end isn't too painful. There is one last thing you can do for her, though.'

'What's that?'

'Take her to the sea.'

'The sea?' Grady frowns. 'Why would Meg want to go there? She can barely walk. And the way she is at the moment, it'd take a two-day drive to get there.'

'She's always wanted to go.'

'Why didn't she ask me?'

'I think she did, but you didn't listen.'

'I suppose over the years there are a lot of things I didn't hear.'

'Or wouldn't.' Connie nods. 'The sea was where she was headed on the day of the accident.'

Grady is silent for a while.

'You could take her there, surprise her,' she adds. 'It would be one last gift.'

The following day, Connie comes to the house Meg and Grady share. She helps Meg from the bed, showers and dresses her. 'Now,' she says briskly to stem the threatening tears. 'Let's pack.'

'Where are we going?' asks Meg.

'Wait and see. It's a surprise.'

Towards the end, when she knows the rest of her life is measured only in weeks, not months, Meg writes a letter to Gemma. Later she seals it in an envelope and hands to Connie.

'Give this to my daughter,' she says, 'when she's old enough to understand. After Grady's gone, tell her the truth about where she came from, and why.'

In the bottom of one of her dressing table drawers, she places a copy of the song she and Declan wrote together, the stubs of two candles and the piece of agate.

She's lost weight – she can tell by looking in the mirror and by the way her skin and clothes hang shapelessly on her. She can barely walk. The medication causes nausea, although it gives her some relief. Her hair has become lifeless and dull. Her skin is tinged with blue.

'We're going on a holiday,' Grady announces, but she feels so tired, so damned exhausted, that she can barely summon any enthusiasm.

'You go without me,' she says. 'Take Gemma instead.'

But Grady shakes his head.

The four of them travel for two stop-start days, across undulating countryside and through seemingly endless wheat fields and paddocks where the grass grows high. They stop frequently so she can rest in the shade of the car. But when she sleeps, or tries to, she can still feel the rocking, the swaying motion of the car, and feels sick.

The Country Singer

Eventually there are hills and valleys, and a wider ribbon of grey tar that winds through them. Then intersecting roads that all seem to lead east, towards the ocean.

Grady has booked a small cottage by the sea. There are three bedrooms and a living room, a tiny kitchen. Meg rests by the living room window, her eyes drawn repeatedly to the view. The sea! She can't believe she's finally here.

Later, they walk down to the shoreline. Gemma runs ahead, Connie following in her wake. Grady carries Meg. 'You're weightless,' he says, holding her gently. 'You need to eat more, keep your strength up.'

She gives him a sad smile.

He lowers her to her feet, at the spot where the land ends and the water begins, supporting her with one arm. Meg feels the sand all gritty and coarse between her toes. The water is cold and she pulls her feet back. Then Grady settles her on a blanket on the dry sand above the high tide mark. His eyes follow Connie and Gemma's progress.

'Will you be all right for a few minutes?' he asks, worry etched on his face.

'Go. I'll be fine,'

She watches him walk towards Gemma and Connie. He is, she thinks, in many ways a special man, made more so by his acceptance of what has happened.

She looks out at the hazy horizon, to the point where the sky runs into the water. She watches that same water run in foamy rivulets up the sand. In the wavy imprint it leaves she can almost imagine Declan's face. 'I'll always love you,' she whispers, and her words are caught by the wind, flung skywards and lost in the blue.

She looks at Grady and Gemma hunting for shells at the water's edge, and knows that somehow they'll be all right after she's gone. Although Grady's genes aren't her daughter's, the pair share something else that matters just as much: a special bond of love that isn't measured by genetics or birthright, but by parenting and care.

Grady comes back and carries her to the cottage. She sits by the window again, looking out over the flat blueness of the ocean. But it means nothing without Declan. She can see Gemma playing on the sand with Connie beside her. Grady is walking slowly back to them, and Meg is tired, so tired, that she can scarcely keep her eyes open…

It is there, in that cottage by the sea, that she dies a few days later.

Grady and Gemma are walking on the beach. Connie is sitting beside her sister-in-law, holding her hand. She hears Meg's rapid breath and watches the shallow rise and fall of her chest. Then – nothing.

'Please, God,' she whispers, hoping that Meg's suffering might be over, yet not wanting to let go either.

For a few minutes, she sits, head bowed, saying a prayer to whoever might listen. Then she beckons Grady from the sand below.

'She's gone,' Connie whispers. Her brother's eyes fill with tears.

The Country Singer

'I loved her. I always loved her.' His voice is choked with emotion. 'But I know she never loved me. It was habit, I guess.' He stares down at his grease-stained hands and fingernails bitten down to the quick. 'She married me out of habit.'

'Grady!' Connie protests quietly, thinking he shouldn't say these things. They're too personal, too raw. But he can't be stopped.

'She must have loved that guy – Declan – to want to leave with him. It hit her real hard, the accident, I know that now. And afterwards I knew I'd lost her. She didn't want to be here, with me.'

'But she *did* stay.'

He's quiet for a while, biting his lip. 'Then,' he goes on, with a rush, as though unable to stop the words escaping. 'When she found out about the baby she was scared, but excited. We'd lost so many before.'

'Grady, about Gemma – '

'I know she isn't mine,' he interrupts her quietly. 'I can see it in her face, her eyes. Anyway, Meg and I hadn't been together, not in that way, for a long time before.'

Connie nods. She knows this is the truth.

He glances through the window at his daughter, who is kneeling just above the high tide mark, building a sandcastle. 'But I love her and she'll always be like a daughter to me.'

He slumps forward, bringing his elbows onto the table as he buries his face in his hands. His shoulders shake as the tears flow. Great wracking sobs come from his mouth.

Connie is powerless to move. She sits there, her eyes lowered, unable to watch as he spends his grief. How can she comfort this man? How can she reduce his pain with soothing words and trite reassurances?

Better to let him cry, she thinks, to let him voice his anguish.

Grady and Gemma and Connie stay on at the beach cottage for several weeks, three people bound together by their mutual grief.

When the time comes, Grady takes Meg's ashes down to the shoreline. He scatters them on the wind and watches the grey powder as it drifts and falls like wood smoke. He sees Gemma playing in the sand and knows she doesn't understand what he is doing. She's too young, he reasons, to be told.

'She didn't know,' he says to Connie later. 'She was busy collecting shells and I didn't have the heart to tell her.'

'Where's Mummy?' asks Gemma for the umpteenth time as she sits with Connie on the front step of the cottage by the sea. 'I want my mummy.'

It's almost dark. There's a salt haze in the air, which obscures the far end of the beach and Connie can smell the tang of it. For a moment she doesn't answer, her mind unable to form the words her young niece needs to hear.

'Where's Mummy?' ask Gemma again, her small elfin face turned towards her aunt.

'Mummy's in heaven.'

Gemma wrinkles her brow. 'Where's heaven?'

Connie points to the sky. 'Up there. She's up there with the angels.' It's dusk and she can see the outline of the evening star, bright and clear, up above the line of salt haze.

'See the star?'

Hesitantly, 'Yes.'

'Well, let's pretend the star is Mummy. And when you really miss her, like tonight, you can come outside and look up and she'll be watching over you.'

Gemma blinks and looks away, and Connie's heart breaks yet again.

'Why don't you run inside to Daddy?' she says, blinking back her own tears. 'I'm sure he wants to see his big girl.'

She watches as Gemma runs inside, hears her excited squeal and imagines Grady swinging his daughter high into the air.

They'll be all right, the three of them – she, Grady and Gemma – she knows. Somehow life will go on, just as Meg went on after Declan's death. The world won't stop turning. The sun will continue to rise every morning.

Connie gets up and takes a deep breath, revelling in the smell of the salt air. The sky is darker now, the star brighter.

'Goodbye, Meg,' she says softly before closing the front door behind her and going inside.

CHAPTER 20

Gemma

2005
The wheat fields, Western Australia

'So that's the end of it,' says Connie, sinking back against her pillow. She looks exhausted by the telling of the story, her face pale. She's handed me an envelope. Her instructions are not to open it until I get back to Grady's house. 'It'd be better to be by yourself when you read it,' she cautions.

Her hands pluck nervously at the bed cover as she waits for my reaction. But I am beyond words, almost beyond thought.

'There was nothing anyone could do,' she goes on. 'It was just a horrible, horrible accident. Declan was dead and your mother was cut about the face and arms, but alive. Somehow I managed to get her out of the car and to the hospital. I collected her things too, you know, her suitcase and personal stuff. She and Grady never spoke about it, in all those years afterwards.'

'He knew my mother didn't love him?'

Connie nods. 'But he thought he loved enough for both of them. Then you were born the following year and you gave them such joy.'

I am silent for a moment, busy digesting the implications of Connie's story. 'So Grady wasn't my father,' I say at last.

I think I've known that was the truth from the beginning of her story, but I need her to say the words and confirm the fact.

'No,' she says slowly with a sad smile. 'Grady wasn't your dad, but he loved you as if he was.'

Back at Grady's place, I sit in the kitchen, open the envelope Connie's given me and spread the pages on the table. Then I start to read.

For Gemma,
My darling daughter,

By the time you read this, Aunt Connie will have given you certain information. I know it'll all be a surprise to you, even a shock, but it was always my intention that you know the truth.

In life there are some things that happen unexpectedly, without planning or foresight. There seems no purpose to them at the time, no valid reason for their being. But time tends to put all things into perspective.

It was September 1969 when your father walked into my life and my heart. His name was Declan O'Brien. He was a kind man, honest and true, respectful and loving, and he had a way with words and music that would make your heart weep. I loved him for his warmth and generosity of spirit. I loved him for what he gave me – you!

He died as he lived, a free spirit, on the road. I cried endless tears for him, for the love we'd lost and the fact that you'd never know him. But he's up there in spirit watching over you. When you see a rainbow bright in the sky, think of him.

I just wanted to tell you how much I love you, and how desperately I long to watch you grow into a woman. But that's not possible. There's something growing inside my head – a brain tumour the doctors call it, something dark and threatening that will soon take me from you. They say it's a result of the accident and I can't stop it – no one can. Some days it is all I can do to keep going.

Connie has promised she will be there for you, and for Grady, who has always been a father to you in the most important sense of the word. I've accepted now that I won't be there to see you on your wedding day, when you look at a man with love. And I won't be there to hold your babies and see them smile. But just remember, my darling daughter, I'll always be here in spirit, the brightest star in your night sky…

The Country Singer

I place the letter on the table before me and the ink smudges into a watery blur. I get up and pour myself a glass of water from the kitchen tap, gulp it down. I feel as though I'm drowning.

I understand many things now, events that seemed uncoordinated and wrong in my child's mind. How can I bear to think of the pain my mother suffered? It was there in the monotony of her marriage and the loss of my father, right through to the sad way her own life ended.

I'm aware of the song playing on Grady's radio. Billie Holliday's voice comes out of the speaker, all husky and soft. The sound of the saxophone snakes towards me, full of sorrow as Billie weeps her blues, the notes stealing inside me, taking hold.

I'm suddenly reminded of something Aunt Connie told me earlier and I go to the verandah. The old 78 is in the middle of the pile of rubbish I'm planning to take to the garbage tip tomorrow morning. Carefully I pull it out and slip the record from its cover. The surface is faintly scratched, as though it's been played many times.

The song is finished on the radio and it's replaced by the harsh tones of the announcer. 'And for all you night owls out there, just let us know your special request…'

I dial the number and the phone answers on the third ring. 'Another Billie Holliday,' I say with a rush. 'And the song's called "Don't Explain".'

'Who would you like to dedicate the song to?'

I hesitate for a fraction of a second, preparing to link the names.

'Are you there?' asks the voice on the other end of the line.

'It's for Meg,' I say. 'For Meg and Declan.'

I turn the radio way up loud and sit on the front step, listening to my request. The notes ring pure and whole, dissolving eventually into the night sky. I think of the sound, lost to me now but maybe still continuing on at some other level.

As I listen to the words, I imagine I am my mother dancing along the verandah with Declan. It is thirty-five years ago, in the last September of the 1960s. It's hot and there's a breeze blowing.

I think of all the rainbows I've seen during my life. Rainbows over the wheat fields and city skylines, arced across a Bali beach and the mountains of Nepal. I think of the significance now, and how unaware I was at the time, and how much I took them for granted.

Tomorrow, I think, Grady will be buried in the ground and in a way it'll be an end to this story, a completion.

I blink back fresh tears and gaze upwards. There are clouds scudding across the moon, obliterating then revealing the stars as they pass. I search for that bright star, the one I associated with my mother in those first painful weeks and months after her death.

The memory comes back, blurred around the edges by the passing of too many years. I'm sitting on the step with

Connie at that little cottage on the beach where my mother died, my aunt asking me look up at the sky. At first I can't remember the actual words that she said, only the general drift of them.

'Where's Mummy?' I sob. 'I want my mummy.'

Connie wraps her arms around me. 'Mummy can't come back,' she says after a while, when my sobs subside. 'Mummy's gone to heaven.'

She points to the night sky, to the evening star that burns the brightest. 'See the light up there?'

I nod, my eyes burning.

'That's Mummy. She's up there with the angels.'

Now, as I remember, my feelings come with a rush and I'm openly crying. Crying for such wasted love. Crying for Meg and Declan and for Grady, who wasn't really my father after all.

I bring the palms of my hands to my eyes, trying to stop the flow of tears. On and on I cry, the sobs shaking out of me from down the years, from my distant childhood.

At last the tears ease. I go to the kitchen, take my wallet from my bag and study the photograph of Greg's well-loved face. I see in the lines there the characteristics of the children we might one day have, the babies that Greg so desperately longs for. 'Marry me,' he'd said on our last night together. 'I won't ask again.'

Greg? What's happening to us?

I think of Meg, my mother, and how she'd lost Declan, the only man she'd ever loved. I consider the possibility of myself growing old, alone.

Now I regret asking Greg not to come to Grady's funeral. If he's to be part of the rest of my life, he should be here to share tomorrow's pain. But it's too late now. Even if I called and told him I'd changed my mind, there's no way he could make it in time.

But when I do see him, back in the city, I'll hug him and hold him tight. I'll tell him yes, that I'd be honoured to be his wife and the mother of his children. I'll tell him how much I love him, and how scared I've been of admitting that to him, scared of giving myself wholly in case part of me, that most vulnerable soft inner core, is somehow snatched away.

I gaze up at the September moon, a hint of silver against the otherwise black sky, and the words rise faint in my mind.

A moment, a fragment,
split second of time.
A dead love, a lost love,
a step out of rhyme

The next morning dawns fine and hot. The funeral's not until after lunch, so I go to the hospital and make arrangements to take Connie out for the few hours we'll need. Then I walk down to the local cemetery.

I know my mother isn't buried there – her ashes were scattered at sea when she died. But Connie has told me where Declan's grave is and I need to see it for myself and pay my respects.

The grave isn't hard to find among the several dozen there. On the mound of weedy earth sits a vase containing a limp bunch of red roses. I recognise them from Aunt Connie's garden.

I sit there for what seems like a long time, thinking. Was Connie a little in love with my real father? I wonder. Was that why she never married? Did she resent my mother, just a bit, for experiencing what she herself had been denied?

A shadow falls over me and I glance up, my thoughts fleeing. It's Greg.

'I know everything. Connie told me,' he says simply.

I stand up and hold him tight, as I promised myself I would. I feel how solid he is, the way he wraps his arms around me as if there's no tomorrow.

'My mother used to come here,' I tell him when I draw away.

'Did she come here to remember, or to forget?'

I shrug. I don't know. My eyes fill with tears. 'It must have been hard, so hard.'

'Gem,' he says, his voice barely a sigh. He holds out his arms again and it feels safe there, secure, and I never want to leave.

'I've missed you, missed us,' I say into the warm side of his neck.

He smells faintly of after-shave and dust. He's come such a long, long way. For me. For us. For what we are together and, I hope, what we're about to become. I'll go back to the city with him, the day after tomorrow, and we'll start planning the rest of our lives. I have so much to catch up on, and so much left undone.

There's also "Meg's Song" and later, when the time is right, I'll show it to him. Maybe I can do a special recording, turn it into a living memory.

The poetry is yours, Declan wrote on the bottom of my copy.

The tune is mine.

I've blended them with love.

ABOUT THE AUTHOR

Robyn Lee Burrows was born and raised in the north-western New South Wales town of Bourke, but has since settled in the Gold Coast hinterland. Her first published books were histories of the local area and they introduced her to what would become a long-standing love of researching all things old – and the challenge, in writing, of putting together a large and complicated jigsaw puzzle. She was hooked and went on to write her first three Australian historical novels: *When Hope is Strong* (1995), *Where the River Ends* (1996) and *Song from the Heart* (1997).

Since then, Robyn has written a biography of Henry Lawson *(Henry Lawson: A Stranger on the Darling)* with her late father, and several bestsellers, including *When Wattles Bloom*, which has been reprinted twice, *Tea-Tree Passage* and *West of the Blue Gums*. Robyn has three adult sons, who finally grew up and left home, and in her seemingly meagre portion of spare time she enjoys pen and ink drawing, watching good movies, dining out and, naturally, reading.

Woman's Day Fiction

Introducing a fabulous new fiction series from
Australia's leading weekly women's magazine,
Woman's Day.
All the books in the series are designed for light
and easy reading and have been written by some of
Australia's leading fiction writers.

Look out for these titles on sale now

ONCE YOU KNOW
By Bunty Avieson

THE COUNTRY SINGER
By Robyn Lee Burrows

coming soon

WHISPERS FROM THE PAST
by Lilly Sommers

THE TOPAZ BROOCH
by Lynne Wilding

Titles in the Woman's Day Fiction series
are available at selected newsagents nationally or
you can order your copy on line at
www.womansday.ninemsn.com.au

Just $9.95

Extract from another title in the Woman's Day Fiction series, *Once You Know*, by Bunty Avieson, on sale now.

CHAPTER 1

Thursday 16th October, 1997

Thomas Libardi checked his watch, then downed his coffee in four noisy gulps. He didn't want to be late for Camille Daintree. There was something about the lonely French lady next door that made him reluctant to let her down.

It was to do with her manner. Camille assumed people would treat her with respect and deference – and they did. Thomas was one of them. He was partly in awe of the enigmatic widow whose nature strip he shared.

To him, Camille had class. Even in her sixties she was one stylish dame. And he loved the way she spoke. Half singing, half breathing her words.

He had bought the house next door nine years ago and had quickly become friendly with her and her husband Philip, who was an academic at Sydney University. He and Thomas often shared a beer on the Daintrees' verandah or in Thomas's garden. A highly respected scholar, Philip was knowledgeable on a range of topics and it always made for an interesting discussion.

Since Philip's death a year ago Thomas had continued to look out for Camille, doing odd jobs, and helping where he could. He fixed the side gate when the screws worked their way out of the hinges and redirected her antenna after a particularly bad hail storm. He remembered the delightfully silly afternoon he had spent on top of the roof, poking the antenna this way and that, while Camille popped her head out of the sitting room window every few minutes to report loudly in her accented English what was happening to the snow on the screen. They got it right eventually. A week later Camille heard from the local Italian grocer that she could watch European movies on cable TV and she had it installed. She never needed the antenna again.

Thomas was expected at 8.30 this morning and was relieved that he was exactly on time when he rang the doorbell. Camille's cat appeared and stood a few feet away eyeing him. She was fat and white and spent as much time in Thomas's garden as she did at home. He called to her, but she stayed where she was.

'What's up, Pusscat?' he said, but she ran off.

Thomas waited for a moment, then rang the doorbell again. The chattering of a pair of birds on the powerlines was the only sound in the quiet suburban street. After a few minutes he pushed open the door.

'Camille?' he called.

The dark hallway was oppressively quiet. It felt strange, unnatural. Thomas had the uncomfortable sensation that something wasn't right.

He stepped carefully inside, his eyes taking a moment to adjust to the gloom.

'Camille,' he called again.

There was no answer. He left the front door wide open and could see that Pusscat had reappeared. She sat very still on the front doormat, watching him, but her eyes told him nothing.

He walked the length of the hallway, looking in the sitting room and the kitchen, but there was no sign of Camille. The back door was locked but Thomas knew she seldom ventured outside. After Philip died she had lost all interest in his garden. She couldn't bear to go out there and refused any offer from Thomas to help tidy it up.

He walked back up the hallway and pushed open the bedroom door. The sight was so unexpected that it took a moment for him to register what he was seeing. Camille was lying on her back on top of the duvet with her eyes closed and her arms by her sides. She was wearing a long coffee-coloured nightgown that covered her from her shoulders to her ankles.

The overhead light was on and cast an artificial glow over the dead woman's features. As rigor mortis had set in, the muscles had stretched the skin, reducing the wrinkles and making it look as if she was smiling. Or perhaps in her final moments she had, in fact, found bliss.

Her hair looked like a platinum blonde halo. It was freshly brushed and arranged, just so. The nightgown looked expensive and could have been fifty years old or bought yesterday. Whatever its age, it was exceptionally luxurious. Her feet were bare, with fresh red nail polish on the toes

Thomas backed slowly out of the room and down the hallway. A lump appeared in his throat that he tried to swallow away.

Outside the sunshine was bright and the birds went on with their chatter. The cat just sat there and looked, her huge green eyes seeming to implore him.

Thomas sank heavily into one of the wicker chairs on the verandah. He had never seen a dead body before and he was profoundly shocked. The Camille he had spoken to half a day earlier had been so vibrant and alive; this Camille was the same and yet so different. The change was immense, but intangible.

His hands were shaking as he pulled his mobile phone from his shirt pocket. What do you do when you find your neighbour dead? Who do you call?

Then he snapped into action. He had lived in the inner Sydney suburb of Leichhardt all his life and knew by heart the number for the local police. The officer who took his call was efficient and businesslike as she recorded all his details and Camille's name and address. She told him to stay where he was, not to touch anything and assured him that a police unit would be there as soon as possible.

Sergeant Mather was a short, round woman in her thirties with cool green eyes that darted about, registering everything. Her manner was authoritative, but with an underlying sympathy.

While Thomas appraised her, he was aware that she was appraising him. He wondered what she saw. Shell-shocked neighbour in his mid-thirties. Obviously never seen a dead body before. Second generation Australian, his family from Italy. Spent a lot of time outdoors and worked with his hands. Thomas was uncomfortably aware of his dirty fingernails.

'Why don't we sit here?' said Sergeant Mather, gesturing to the wicker armchairs.

He watched her sit down and took the seat opposite, with his back to the sitting room window and a view across the quiet suburban road.

'Just tell me in your own words what happened.' She opened her notebook and waited for him to start.

Thomas spoke slowly and carefully, trying to describe everything exactly as it had unfolded. 'I rang the doorbell and when there was no answer I pushed it open. I had a funny feeling that something wasn't right. There was a mood to the house that I can't really describe; not empty exactly, but as if it was waiting. I know that doesn't make sense, but I can't think of any other way to describe it. It's like when you hit the pause button on a cd. It's not finished; it's just on hold, in limbo. That's what the house felt like when I walked in.

'The wardrobe that Mrs Daintree wanted me to fix was in her bedroom, so after I couldn't find her anywhere else, I put my head in there – and that's when I saw her. She looked amazing. I knew straightaway she was dead rather than sleeping. Mrs Daintree just wasn't there, in that body. It was empty.

'"She" – whatever that word takes in – had "gone". The real essence of Mrs Daintree had left the building.'

Sergeant Mather stopped taking notes and listened with understanding. She remembered her first corpse. It had been a woman her own age, beaten black and blue. That image would never leave her. Death was unnerving in whatever form it came. She shared her thoughts with Thomas, empathising with him, and he started to relax.

He looked back at the front door, every detail stark in his mind.

'I still can't get my head around it. Mrs Daintree was as friendly and "buoyant" as ever at six o'clock last night… And then her dead body this morning. It was such a dramatic difference. In one way it was still her. She looked exactly the same. Elegant, even like that.'

Sergeant Mather looked at her pad. 'That was at 8.30am?'

'Yes. Then I called you. I guess it would have been about two minutes after I arrived at the house and found her. I didn't touch anything. I felt a bit awkward being in the house after Mrs Daintree had died and I didn't like to make myself comfortable because that seemed rude. I didn't even feel I should make a cup of coffee, though I knew Mrs Daintree wouldn't have minded.

'So I just sat here on the front verandah and waited for you to come.'

Sergeant Mather checked her watch and wrote down the time.

'You obviously knew her well…'

'Why do you say that?'

The question made him nervous. He appeared agitated and he knew it. But she didn't seem unduly concerned. Thomas supposed most people were uncomfortable around death, or perhaps the people she normally dealt with in a day were nervous around a police uniform. She spoke kindly, but looked him directly in the eye.

'When no one answered the door, you pushed it open and went inside. That sounds to me like someone who was pretty well known to the occupant, wouldn't you say?'

Thomas felt relieved. 'Camille was expecting me to come and fix her wardrobe this morning. She told me the creaky hinge was scaring her cat. When she didn't answer the door, I thought she was probably in the kitchen and couldn't hear me, so I came in.'

'And the door was unlocked?'

'Yes.'

Sergeant Mather nodded, but stayed silent, looking at Thomas, waiting for him to fill the void.

Too smart for that old trick, he stared straight back. He

was a TV cop show fan and thought he knew what she was up to.

'Tell me about Mrs Daintree,' she suggested finally.

He described the past nine years, how he had become friendly with the couple next door. He knew Philip better, as they shared a love of gardening, but had always admired and respected Camille.

'She was a lovely woman, if a bit lonely. French. Never one to go out and get the mail in her dressing gown, if you know what I mean. She used to like to watch the old French movies on cable. I do too, so we used to talk about them sometimes.'

He spoke with respect and affection and the expression in his eyes matched his face and tone of voice. Sergeant Mather figured that, on balance, he was probably exactly as he presented himself – the shocked next-door neighbour.

'Did she have any visitors last night? Did you hear any noises coming from her house?'

Thomas shook his head. 'I saw her at about six when I put out my bins and then I went out and didn't get home until about eleven. I went straight to bed. I didn't hear anything.'

'When did Mr Daintree die?'

'Fifteenth of October last year. I remember because it was on my sister Petra's fiftieth birthday. We had a big family party in my garden. Philip died of a heart attack. It was very sudden. We heard the ambulance...'

'A year ago yesterday,' said Sergeant Mather. 'That's interesting.'

'I hadn't thought of that,' said Thomas. 'How sad.'

'Apart from the husband, did Mrs Daintree have any other family?'

'There is a daughter, Jacqueline. She works for a law firm in Melbourne. Her father was very proud of her, though Mrs Daintree didn't mention her much. Some sort of bad feeling there. I don't know why. Mrs Daintree was such a lovely woman. It makes me sad to think of her dying alone like that with only me to notice.'

An ambulance officer called out to the sergeant and she excused herself, leaving Thomas alone with his thoughts. Pusscat reappeared, wrapped herself around his legs and moaned. She made no attempt to go inside the house.

'Looks like you'll be coming with me,' said Thomas. 'Poor little thing. We're going to miss your French mistress, aren't we?' He sat forward in the wicker armchair, straining to hear what was being said inside.

It was dark inside the house. The warmth of the spring morning had not penetrated the brick walls and it was cool, like a vault.

Sergeant Mather followed the ambulance officer into the bedroom where a police constable was making notes on his own little pad. The room was elegantly decorated with a huge antique bed.

She looked with dispassionate interest at the body laid out so elegantly on the bed. She took in the expensive nightgown, the freshly brushed hair and the vivid red of her bare toes.

'She's a good looking corpse,' said the ambulance officer, a young man in his twenties. 'The best I've seen in a long time.'

Sergeant Mather agreed. 'For a woman living on her own, she's gone to a lot of trouble to get ready for bed.'

'Do you think she was expecting a lover?' he asked.

Sergeant Mather raised an eyebrow. 'Settle, Roger. Mind on the job, please. Now tell me why you called me in. What am I looking for?'

The constable took over, pointing to the bedside table. There was an antique pearl-backed hairbrush. A leather-bound book. A small plastic container of pills. She bent down and read the label. Common prescription sleeping pills. The date was the day before. The container was empty.

Her foot brushed something hard as she moved and she heard the clink of glass. An open bottle of Louis Roederer Cristal champagne was tucked away discreetly behind the bedside table leg and lying next to it was a glass. She lifted the hem of the duvet to look under the bed for another, but the space was filled with boxes. She turned to the constable.

'One glass?'

'Looks like it,' he said. 'There is another one on the sink in the kitchen, but it's been washed. I can't tell whether it was used recently or not.'

The sergeant inspected the bottle. It was two-thirds full. She stepped carefully over it to the wardrobe. The doors opened and closed with a quiet but audible click. The left one was stiff with a loose hinge but it appeared to have been that way for a long time. Why the need to get it fixed now? she wondered. Maybe she *had* been concerned about her cat – but then again, maybe she had another reason for arranging Thomas's visit that morning.

'What do you think?' asked the constable.

'I think Camille Daintree is a class act. I'm only guessing at this stage, but I would say that she was grief stricken for her late husband and has decided to go and join him. Look at her. She has gone to so much trouble, it could be her wedding night. And I'm thinking our French lady may be a touch vain. To ensure her body doesn't rot away in here, she has organised for the next-door neighbour to find her. Vain and smart. My kind of woman.'

She put her notebook in her jacket pocket and turned to leave. 'Looks like suicide to me, but let's do it by the book. Get the coroner here.'

Woman's Day Fiction

THE TOPAZ BROOCH
BY LYNNE WILDING

When Irish jeweller Liam Westaway makes a topaz brooch for Corinne, the woman he loves, he doesn't realise how much his life will change. Liam's gypsy mother has put an enchantment on the brooch - *who wears it will find true love.* Over three generations, and half way across the world and back again, the brooch exerts its mystical power - over Liam and Corinne, brutally separated by her father, the earl; through wartime Sydney when a beautiful young girl sees a broken brooch in the gutter and picks it up; and for a strong-willed '70s wildchild who follows her love to Europe.

On sale March 2005

Woman's Day Fiction

WHISPERS FROM THE PAST
BY LILLY SOMMERS

It is 1928 and, after the death of her beloved husband Billy, Evie Woodward and her husband's best friend, Daniel Roxburgh, are partners in the Roxburgh Psychic Detective Agency, a bogus agency supposedly investigating psychic phenomena. When Evie channels a French woman Genevieve from beyond the grave, it is as if a pin is pulled from her life and the truth begins to unravel. She arrives at the manor house Blue Waters and has the uneasy feeling she is holding the end of the thread, but may be bound up in the past much more tightly than she thinks...

On sale April 2005